A GHOUL NAMED GATZ

Major Mortimer Gatz might be an officer—but he didn't even pretend to be a gentleman. Giving a man a sporting chance wasn't the way he played the game, and a ghoulish grin lit his face as he watched his squad of soldiers teach Skye Fargo a lesson in pure pain.

By now Fargo was only able to croak through split lips, "Only a coward lets others do his dirty work."

"Finish him, Private Jenkins," the major commanded.

"My pleasure, sir," the man-mountain of a soldier responded, and moved forward to deliver the final savage blow as Skye Fargo panted on his hands and knees, too weak to rise.

"Just kneel there a moment longer and it will all be over," Jenkins said as he raised his huge stony fist.

The Trailsman didn't figure it could get worse than this.

He was wrong.

THE TRAILSMAN

187

SIOUX WAR CRY

by

Jon Sharpe

Ⓢ

A SIGNET BOOK

SIGNET
Published by the Penguin Group
Penguin Books USA Inc., 375 Hudson Street,
New York, New York 10014, U.S.A.
Penguin Books Ltd, 27 Wrights Lane,
London W8 5TZ, England
Penguin Books Australia Ltd,
Ringwood, Victoria, Australia
Penguin Books Canada Ltd, 10 Alcorn Avenue,
Toronto, Ontario, Canada M4V 3B2
Penguin Books (N.Z.) Ltd, 182–190 Wairau Road,
Auckland 10, New Zealand

Penguin Books Ltd, Registered Offices:
Harmondsworth, Middlesex, England

First published by Signet, an imprint of Dutton Signet,
a division of Penguin Books USA Inc.

First Printing, July, 1997
10 9 8 7 6 5 4 3 2 1

The first chapter of this book originally appeared in *Blue Sierra Renegades*,
the one hundred eighty-sixth volume in this series.

 REGISTERED TRADEMARK—MARCA REGISTRADA

Printed in the United States of America

The Trailsman

Beginnings . . . they bend the tree and they mark the man. Skye Fargo was born when he was eighteen. Terror was his midwife, vengeance his first cry. Killing spawned Skye Fargo, ruthless, cold-blooded murder. Out of the acrid smoke of gunpowder still hanging in the air, he rose, cried out a promise never forgotten.

The Trailsman they began to call him all across the West: searcher, scout, hunter, the man who could see where others only looked, his skills for hire but not his soul, the man who lived each day to the fullest, yet trailed each tomorrow. Skye Fargo, the Trailsman, and the seeker who could take the wildness of a land and the wanting of a woman and make them his own.

1861—northern Minnesota,
where bigotry raged like a wildfire,
blood rained in a downpour,
and the innocent were unwary victims. . . .

1

Skye Fargo was about a mile out from Fort Snelling when the madwoman nearly killed him.

The big man with the steely lake-blue eyes had stopped at noon to give the Ovaro a brief rest. They had been pushing hard for over a week, heading out before first light each morning, and riding until late at night. Both of them were showing signs of fatigue. So when Fargo rounded a bend and saw a grassy clearing to the left of the trail, he reined up and allowed the Ovaro to graze.

The rutted excuse for a road was heavily used. Settlers had been streaming into the region ever since the federal government opened land west of the Mississippi River for settlements a few years back. Many lumberjacks were among them, bound for the growing new communities of Minneapolis and St. Anthony.

Several heavily laden wagons filled with noisy families, as well as occasional riders, passed Fargo as he sat propped against a stump, letting the sun warm him. The mornings were brisk in Minnesota at that time of year, and he welcomed the heat the afternoon would bring.

A knot of lumbermen leading pack mules had gone by a few minutes ago. In the quiet that followed, Fargo could hear a robin chirping in the pines behind him and chipmunks chattering in a nearby cluster of boulders. Overhead, a flock of ducks winged westward.

Fargo smiled. The sights and sounds of the wilderness never failed to have a soothing effect on him, and he felt his tense muscles relaxing. He was as much at home in the deep woods as most men were in a city or town.

Reaching up to push his hat brim back, Fargo suddenly froze. His skin prickled as it sometimes did when he was being observed by unseen eyes. Instinctively, he swiveled toward the bend.

Astride a fine bay sat a lanky man dressed in a black frock coat and a wide-brimmed black hat, the sort of garb favored by riverboat gamblers and the like. But no gambler alive had ever been able to ride up close to Fargo unnoticed. It was a feat worthy of an Apache or Sioux warrior.

Fargo studied the man closely while being studied in turn. Where he had a beard, the stranger was clean shaven. Where his dark mane of hair fell to his shoulders, the stranger's sandy hair had been cropped close and trimmed around the ears. Dark eyes met his evenly.

"Howdy," the man said in a voice as deep as Fargo's own. "You wouldn't happen to know how much farther it is to Minneapolis, would you?"

"A mile or so," Fargo answered, resting his right hand on his thigh, close to his Colt.

The corners of the stranger's thin lips quirked upward. "Not the trusting type, are you, friend?"

Fargo shook his head. "I find that I live longer that way. "In these parts too much trust can get a man killed."

"I know what you mean." The stranger's grin widened. "Reminds me of my grandfather's favorite saying." He paused. "Love thy neighbor, but never go anywhere without your gun."

Despite himself, Fargo laughed. His intuition told him that the man in black posed no threat. Yet at the same time, he was sure there was a lot more to the rider than met the eye. The next moment the man shifted to squint up at the sun, and the frock coat parted. Around the rider's waist was a wide red sash. Jutting from the top of it, butt forward, was a pearl-handled, ivory-plated Remington. "Nice pistol you have there."

"It hits what I aim at," the stranger allowed. Kneeing the bay forward, he said, "Well, nice meeting you. If you stop in Minneapolis and don't mind losing at cards, look me up. My name is Ethan Lee."

"If I do, I won't be the one who loses," Fargo said.

Lee found that amusing. "I respect a gent with confidence, even if he is a mite misguided." Touching his hat brim, he applied his spurs and was soon lost to view around the next turn to the north.

Fargo settled back to rest. The creak of wagon wheels in dire need of grease and the snorts of a plodding team heralded new arrivals. Presently, another family of settlers appeared. Husband and wife were perched on the seat, both wearing homespun clothes that had seen better days. In the wagon was their raucous brood, five or six kids from the sound of things, all of them yelling and squealing and bickering at once.

The husband, a burly specimen who looked to be as strong as one of his oxen, spied the clearing and veered toward it. "Hello there!" he hollered to be heard above the racket. "Hope you don't mind if we stop here a spell. My animals are tuckered out, and we need to stretch our legs."

Fargo could take a hint. Sighing, he rose and said, "Feel free. I was just leaving anyway." He walked to the Ovaro as the wagon rattled to a stop. Six grubby faces poked out and peered at him.

"It isn't far to Minneapolis, is it?" the husband inquired hopefully.

"Someone should post a sign," Fargo muttered, stepping into the stirrups.

"Pardon?"

"No, not far at all," Fargo revealed. "You'll be there within the hour." He glanced at the weary team and saw the top of an iron stove mixed in with the belongings crammed into the bed. "Maybe two, as filled as you are."

The husband let out with a howl of pure delight. "Did

you hear that, Maude? We're almost there! After three whole months, we're almost to our new home!"

Yips of delight burst from the children. The man went on howling like a demented wolf as Fargo swung toward the trail. They were making so much noise that he did not realize another wagon was coming up behind them until it swept around the bend. He looked up just as it appeared, and saw four lathered mules flying toward him at breakneck speed, being lashed on by a figure who flicked a bullwhip in cracking cadence.

"Out of the way, you damned idiot!" the figure bawled, making no attempt to stop or swerve.

The settler's wife screamed. So did several of her children.

Fargo hauled on the reins for all he was worth, cutting the pinto to the right to get out of the way. Normally steady of nerves and as dependable as gold, the Ovaro shied, rearing and plunging. The team flew past. It missed them by the width of a whisker, the rumbling of the wheels like the peal of thunder. Fargo glimpsed a beaming face, a shapely form in buckskins, and streaming red tresses.

Maybe it was being caught unaware by the Ovaro. Maybe it was the shock of seeing the driver was a woman. Or maybe it was both combined that caused Fargo to suffer a mishap he rarely did. He was thrown.

The sky and the ground exchanged places. Trees were abruptly upside down. His hat went one direction, and he went another. Then Fargo thudded onto his left shoulder, grimacing at pain that seared down his arm and spine. Dazed, he rolled onto his back and saw clouds spinning above him. Dimly, he heard footsteps rushing to his side. Grubby faces replaced the clouds.

"Stand back, kids! Give me room!" the settler bellowed.

Strong hands helped Fargo to sit up. He winced, his left shoulder tingling.

"Are you all right, mister?" the settler's wife asked, genuinely concerned. "I was afraid you'd split your skull open."

"That was a freight wagon," the husband noted, coughing as the cloud of dust raised by its passage wafted down over them. "Going like a bat out of hell, too."

"Harvey!" Maude said. "Watch your language when the children are present."

The settler was too excited to heed. "Did you see that female on top handle that whip of hers? Damn, she could make it sing!"

Someone placed Fargo's hat on his head, and he was boosted erect. His head clearing, he saw the Ovaro standing quietly now, head hung low as if ashamed of its antics. Fargo shrugged himself clear and straightened. "Thanks for the help," he said, anger swelling within him like the wind in a rising storm. Stalking to the stallion, he quickly mounted, jabbed his spurs into its flanks, and was off like a cannon shot, galloping hard in pursuit.

It galled Fargo that the woman had nearly ridden him down. They were a notorious lot, the freighters: tough, rowdy, and as arrogant as the day was long. Most acted as if roads had been invented just so they could barrel down them at speeds no sane person would dare go.

The thick dust prevented Fargo from catching sight of his quarry. He went around the turn to the north, raced along a straight stretch hundreds of yards long, and on around the base of a low hill. Up ahead someone hollered. A horse whinnied, and a string of lusty oaths told Fargo that someone else had suffered the same fate he had.

Sure enough, once past the next bend Fargo saw the man in black in the act of standing. Ethan Lee, flushed with anger, shook a fist in the air. Another flurry of curses were hurled at the redhead, who had already vanished. There was no sign of the bay.

Lee turned as the Ovaro approached. Brushing off his sleeves, he growled, "Hello again, friend. You won't believe this, but a hellcat on a freight wagon nearly just trampled me to death."

"I believe it," Fargo said, drawing rein. "She did the same thing to me."

"Really?" Lee's color deepened. "When I catch up with that woman, I'm going to strangle her with those red locks of hers." Sticking two fingers into his mouth, he uttered a piercing whistle. Soon, from out of the woods, trotted his horse, reins dangling. "It's downright embarrassing. She spooked my animal so bad, he threw me. That's never happened before."

"Then, we have something else in common," Fargo disclosed. Lee looked at him, and suddenly, although Fargo could not quite say why, the pair of them were laughing heartily.

"I'd hate to be that hellcat's husband," Lee commented as he forked leather. "She probably cracks her whip over him as much as she does her mules."

They rode on side by side. Fargo did not push to catch up to the freighter. Now that his anger had subsided, there was no need. Minneapolis was not very big. He'd find the troublemaker soon enough.

Removing his bandanna, Fargo wiped dirt from his cheek and neck. He thought of the dispatch in his saddlebags, which was responsible for his being there, and wondered if the officer who sent it had been misinformed.

Captain Jim Beckworth was career Army. A competent, dedicated soldier, he had worked his way up the ranks while stationed at a variety of frontier posts.

A year ago, while crossing the prairie, Fargo had stumbled on Beckworth's cavalry patrol trapped in a gully by a small band of marauding Arapahoes. He had winged the leader of the war party, causing them to scatter. In gratitude, Beckworth had treated Fargo to a night of whiskey, women, and bawdy times that left Fargo with the world's worst hangover. They had not seen each other since.

Eight days ago, out of the blue, a message had caught up

with him in Denver. It had been short and to the point: *"Come quick. Sioux uprising feared. Hundreds may die without your help."* It had been sent by Beckworth from Fort Snelling in Minnesota.

So far, though, Fargo had seen no sign of the Sioux, nor any evidence of the other Indian tribes known to inhabit the region. None of the travelers and locals he met had expressed any worry about an uprising. Everything appeared to be tranquil.

As if Ethan Lee were privy to Fargo's thoughts, the gambler mentioned casually, "You haven't happened to come across any sign of the Sioux in your travels, have you? Down in St. Louis, I heard tell that they've been making some trouble up this way." Lee plucked a spotless white handkerchief from his shirt pocket and commenced cleaning his own face.

"No, I haven't," Fargo said.

Ethan Lee sighed. "I hope to hell the rumors aren't true. There will be the devil to pay if they ever go on the warpath. Especially if most of the federal troops are sent East, as the newspapers are saying they might be."

Fargo was familiar with the accounts. Trouble was brewing between Northern states and Southern states over the issue of slavery. Some experts were predicting it would lead to war. People living on the frontier were worried that if hostilities did break out, all government troops would be called back to deal with the crisis, leaving wilderness outposts vulnerable to attacks by hostile Indians.

"I didn't catch your handle, by the way," Lee commented.

Fargo told him. His name was fairly well known west of the Mississippi, so he was not surprised when the gambler responded with "Interesting," and let it go at that.

Presently, they caught up with a party of loggers who were collecting horses that had scattered into the trees on either side of the road. A beefy man holding a bloody arm at his side spotted them and pointed toward Minneapolis.

"Any chance of one of you fetching a sawbones for us? I've got a hurt arm, and my partner Ben broke his leg."

Propped against a Norway pine was a lean man whose pants had been sliced open to reveal the wound.

"What happened?" Fargo asked. As if he could not guess.

The logger's jaw muscles twitched. "We were taking some spare horses to our outfit southwest of here when Wagon Annie came racing on down the road. She came close to killing the both of us! One of these days that woman is going to go too far!"

"Wagon Annie? That's what she calls herself?" Ethan Lee said, and chuckled. "If she's such a nuisance, why doesn't someone put her in her place?"

"Are you crazy?" the logger said. "That female doesn't take guff off of anyone. Just try to trim her feathers and she's liable to gut you or peel your skin off an inch at a time with that nasty whip of hers. She's as mean as a stuck snake when she's riled."

"Any woman can be tamed if a man puts his mind to it," Lee asserted.

Fargo knew differently, but he held his tongue. Any man who regarded women as if they were pets had a lot to learn about the female of the species. Some were as wild as mustangs, as willful as grizzlies, and no amount of "taming" was ever going to change them.

"Excuse me," interrupted the logger with the broken leg, "but while you two chuckleheads are jawing away, I'm suffering over here. How about that doctor? I'd like to get the bone reset before the end of the year."

Fargo lifted his reins, prepared to volunteer, but the gambler beat him to it.

"I'll go," Lee said, breaking into a trot. Over his shoulder, he called back, "Nice meeting you, Skye. If we run into each other in town, the drinks will be on me."

Two more loggers came out of the woods, leading horses. They hurried to their stricken companion, one bringing a blanket to spread over him. Since they had the matter well in hand, Fargo rode on. It was not long before he encountered more travelers, including four wagons loaded with settlers. At the rate people were pouring into the region, it wouldn't be long before the Indians were crowded out.

Was that why the Sioux were agitated? Fargo asked himself. It was a pattern repeated again and again, ever since the first colonists came to America. In their never-ending quest for land, whites were slowly but surely forcing the Indians into a literal corner.

Years ago there had been savage warfare in New England and in the southeast part of the country due to this very thing. Now some were of the opinion that more bloodshed could erupt at any time in the West.

Fargo would hate to see that happen. Both sides would suffer terribly, the Indians worst of all. He did not share the commonly held view that the only good Indian was a dead one. In his estimation, they deserved the same fair treatment as everyone else.

Presently, the Ovaro crested a rise. Below unfolded a lush vista of verdant land crisscrossed by winding waterways. On the east side of the broad Mississippi River was St. Anthony, started by a missionary explorer many years before. On the west side sat newer Minneapolis, and Fargo was amazed at how much it had grown since the last time he crossed the territory.

South of Minneapolis stood Fort Snelling. Built on an ideal site, near where the Mississippi and the Minnesota rivers met, one end was flanked by a steep hill for extra protection. As thirsty and hungry and tired as Fargo was, he headed for the fort first instead of the town.

The gate was wide open, and neither of the sentries challenged him. Nor did the soldiers manning the battlements raise a cry. Apparently, anyone was free to come and go as they pleased, so long as they were white. A Winnebago who tried to enter in front of Fargo was turned sternly away.

As military posts went, Snelling had more to offer than most. Officers' quarters were comfortable, the barracks for the enlisted men well insulated against the harsh winter climate. Provisions were seldom scarce thanks to a steady stream of river and freight traffic. Compared to some forts farther west, it was a paradise.

Fargo asked at the adjutant's office about his friend, and learned the captain was at the officers mess. A private was assigned to guide him. It being the middle of the afternoon, few officers were there. Fargo spied Beckworth at a table near the front with another officer. Both were so engrossed in their talk that neither were aware of him until the private snapped to attention and announced crisply, "Colonel Williams, sir! A visitor to see the captain."

Jim Beckworth was a broad-shouldered man with a thick mustache. He leaped out of his chair and clapped Fargo on the arms as he might a long-lost relative. "Skye! You received my message! Thank God, you came!"

Fargo had the dispatch in his right hand. Wagging it, he said with a smile, "This had better be important. I was on a winning streak when it reached me."

The captain swung toward his superior, a portly man who had risen and was smoothing his gray-flecked hair. "Colonel, allow me to introduce the fellow I was telling you about, the only one who can avert the bloodshed we foresee."

Fargo and Williams shook. The private was dismissed. A fresh pot of coffee was brought from the kitchen, and Beckworth poured for all three of them. Colonel Williams offered to have a cook rustle up some food, but Fargo declined. He had tasted Army fare before.

"Well, then, to business," Colonel Williams went on. "Captain Beckworth has told me that you once lived among the Sioux. Is this true?"

"Yes," Fargo confirmed. He felt no need to mention that

it had been a long time ago, and that many of the skills for which he was noted stemmed in large measure from the teachings the Sioux had imparted.

The colonel was immensely pleased. "Then, you are in a unique position to do this nation an invaluable service. The lives of countless innocent homesteaders rest on the decision you make here today."

Fargo took a sip of piping hot coffee while waiting for the commanding officer to get to the point.

"As you might know, we're sitting on a powder keg," Williams detailed. "It's our job to make sure the Winnebagos stay on their reservation, and to protect the settlements in this region from the Chippewas and the Sioux, who have been giving us a great deal of trouble in recent months. Particularly, the Sioux. I'm desperately afraid that the smallest incident will set them off, inciting a full-scale war."

"I don't see how I can be of any help," Fargo said when the man paused and regarded him expectantly. "You must have scouts on your payroll who are more familiar with the area than I am."

Colonel Williams made a teepee of his fingers. "Oh, yes, indeed we do. No, what I had in mind was for you to go talk to the Sioux. Calm their fears. Explain that if they make trouble, they will pay most dearly. That sort of thing."

The tin cup was suspended halfway to Fargo's mouth. "Do you have any idea what you're asking? Why should they listen to me?"

"You've lived with them—" Colonel Williams began.

"With the Tetons, who live hundreds of miles away on the plains," Fargo cut him off. "The Sioux who live here are the Santees. They don't know me from Adam. My word would carry no weight."

Both officers frowned. "But we had such high hopes," Captain Beckworth said, and leaned forward so none of the mess staff could overhear. "You see, Skye, we have reason to suspect that an unknown party is supplying guns to the Santees. With your help, maybe we can put a stop to it."

Just then the same orderly bustled up to the table and addressed the colonel. "Sir! Sorry to disturb you, but Lieutenant Miles urgently requests your presence outside right away. A civilian is causing a disturbance."

"Is that so?" Williams huffed, donning his hat. "Well, whoever it is will soon regret their mistake. Come along, Captain."

Out of curiosity, and to stretch his legs, Fargo trailed them, taking his coffee along. Yells and curses fell on his ears as he strolled through the doorway. That was when he saw Wagon Annie scattering troopers right and left with her bullwhip. Flabbergasted, he stopped—and the tip of the whip streaked toward his face.

2

A bullwhip in the hands of someone who knew how to use it was a formidable weapon. Up to twenty-five feet in length, it was crafted from braided rawhide and could cut through flesh as easily as a razor.

Skye Fargo had a split second in which to react before the tapered tip of Wagon Annie's whip seared into him. In sheer reflex he threw himself to the right and heard the whip whiz past. The tin cup upended, spilling coffee over his legs and onto the steps.

Again the whip snapped, this time an inch from Colonel Williams, halting him in mid-stride. The robust senior officer, who moments ago had been so intent on confronting the culprit, had a change of heart. Adopting a wan smile, he held his hands out from his sides. "I should have known it would be you, Miss Standley. Hold on there before you harm somebody."

"It's Wagon Annie to you, big belly!" the redhead roared as lustily as any saloon brawler who ever lived. "And whether any of your little boys lose some skin depends on whether you fork over the money due me, pronto!"

For the first time Fargo got a good look at the firebrand who qualified as a walking natural disaster. He expected to see a female version of the typical male bull whacker, namely a grungy character in shabby clothes whose aversion to bathing was matched only by her complete lack of any feminine charm.

Instead, Fargo saw a stunning woman whose shapely

contours would be the envy of any woman who ever aspired to be beautiful. Her buckskins were clean and recently made, clinging to her lush figure like a second skin. A fetching brown hat perched rakishly on her lustrous red hair, which cascaded in curls to the middle of her back.

Wagon Annie's face was in itself enough to stir a man's carnal hunger. She had a smooth complexion bronzed by daily exposure to the sun, arched eyebrows that lent her an air of above-average intelligence, a tiny, dainty nose, and red lips so ripe and luscious that it brought to mind fresh cherry pie.

She had a way about her when she moved, too, as if her body were solid but curvy muscle packed in all the right places. When she spun to crack her whip, she displayed a grace and poise that only the finest of dancers possessed. Fearless blue eyes blazed at the ring of troopers, a mocking gleam daring them to close in and taste her lash.

Colonel Williams turned to a subordinate who was gaping at the freighter as if she had just dropped out of the sky from another planet. "Lieutenant Miles, will you kindly explain what has this infernal woman so upset?"

Miles was a youngster, so new to the frontier that his skin was still pale. Composing himself, he said, "Sir, all I did was tell her that the quartermaster went into St. Anthony and would not be back until late this afternoon. I suggested she should come back tomorrow morning to be paid, and she started cursing me roundly in front of the men. When I threatened to have her forcibly removed from the post if she did not comport herself as a lady should, she broke out that toy of hers."

"That toy" sizzled the air, crackling like a gunshot so close to the young lieutenant's ear that he jumped, startled.

"Insult me again, boy, and I'll have your ears for keepsakes!" Wagon Annie thundered. "I'm more of a lady than any gal you've ever met, and that includes the one who suckled you on her teat!"

Fargo choked off budding laughter as the young officer fumed in righteous indignation.

"How dare you! You—you—" Miles sputtered, at a loss for words, finally choosing the worst possible one, "you rowdy bitch, you!"

The whip was a blur. It looped around the lieutenant's ankles and yanked him off his feet so fast that he was flat on the ground before he quite knew what had happened.

Wagon Annie jerked the lash back with a crisp snap of her wrist. Her features were ablaze as she cocked her arm for another blow. "Nobody calls me that, boy! If you weren't such a pathetic excuse for a man, I'd hack off your little—"

Colonel Williams had a voice that could be heard from one end of the post to the other, and he used it now to full effect. "*Enough!* I will abide no more of this childish behavior! Lieutenant Miles, you will go to my office and wait there for me. Obviously, you need to be reminded how an officer and a gentleman properly deports himself."

"But, sir—" Miles protested.

"*Now,* soldier. That was an order, not a request." Williams faced the redheaded fury. "As for you, Miss Standley, you should know better. When has the Army ever failed to pay its bills?"

Wagon Annie was not intimidated. Calmly standing there with her right hip thrust defiantly forward in a provocative pose, she responded, "Oh, it pays its bills, all right, in its own sweet time." She wagged a slender finger. "You're the one who should know better, Fred. I only haul for cash on the barrel head. Always have. Always will. So fork over the money, or you'll have to explain to your superiors how a woman was able to put seven or eight of your men in the hospital before you could subdue her."

Fargo's admiration for the freighter was growing by leaps and bounds. In all his travels, he'd never met a woman with so much grit, certainly never one who could hold off a company of soldiers with such skill and wit. He was almost inclined to overlook how near she had come to crushing him under her wheels. Almost, but not quite.

Colonel Williams was a study in resigned frustration. From his jacket he took a billfold. "How much do we owe you this time around, Annie?"

"Two hundred and sixty-three dollars," the redhead said.

Williams swallowed, then coughed. "I'm afraid I don't usually carry quite that much on my person. Would one hundred and twenty tide you over until the quartermaster returns?"

Fargo saw every man there brace for another slash of the whip, but they misjudged the redheaded hellion. She was no fool. Smiling seductively, she winked at Williams, whose cheeks burned red.

"Tell you what, Fred. Since it's you, and since you asked so nice and all, I'll make an exception this one time only. But don't ever let it happen again or you can rely on someone else to get your urgent freight here on time."

Captain Beckworth leaned toward Fargo, and whispered, "I hate to admit it, but that woman is the best freighter in Minnesota, maybe in the whole West. Rain or shine, blistering hot or freezing cold, she always gets through, and always on schedule. Don't judge her too harshly."

If anything, Fargo was doing the opposite. He admired how her body swayed enticingly as she sashayed up to the colonel for her money. It was a pity that he had to do what he did next, which was to walk over while she was preoccupied counting her cash and to say politely so she would not be forewarned, "Excuse me, ma'am, but I owe you something, too."

Wagon Annie was still counting. "You do?" she said, slowly pivoting. "Who might you be and what do you owe me?"

"This," Fargo said, and slugged her in the gut as hard as he would any man. She folded like a paperboard carton, but she did not go to her knees as most would have. The bills fluttering at her feet, she wheezed and gasped for breath, her lovely face framed by her red curls. "And if you ever try to run me off the road again, I'll keep *your* ears for keepsakes."

So saying, Fargo spun on a boot heel and headed for the mess. The troopers were gawking at him in astonishment. Those who were closest hastily moved elsewhere in case Annie came after him. They need not have bothered. She was still bent over, unable to speak, let alone wield her whip.

Fargo poured himself another cup of coffee and took his seat. He had polished off half of it when the commanding officer and Beckworth entered. Subdued, they sat down and did not say a thing, so Fargo got them back on track. "Tell me more about those rifles you mentioned."

Jim Beckworth cocked his head. "That can wait a minute. Do you realize what you've just done?" He shook his head in disbelief. "You just struck the meanest woman this side of the Rockies. She won't rest until she pays you back, in spades."

"In fact," Colonel Williams continued when the captain stopped, "she asked us to inform you that she'll be waiting for you in Minneapolis when you're done here. At the North Star Saloon."

"Fair enough," Fargo said. Downing the rest of the brew in a single gulp, he set the cup down with a smack. "The rifles," he prodded.

Williams and Beckworth exchanged puzzled expressions. "Very well," the senior officer said. "As we indicated, someone is smuggling guns to the Santees. New Henrys, the very best that money can buy. It makes no sense because the Santees are a poor people. Most of their warriors can barely afford to buy a new knife once a year, let alone a repeater. And all they own worth trading are their horses, which they'd never part with."

Beckworth nodded. "So far only one shipment that we're aware of has gotten through. We heard about it when one of their young warriors, Fire Thunder, made the mistake of bragging to a friendly Winnebago about how the Sioux were going to make the territory run red with white blood. When the Winnebago pointed out that the Sioux stood no chance against our guns and cannons, Fire Thunder crowed about how the Sioux had rifles of their own now, brand-spanking-new Henrys, and how soon they would have many more."

Fargo could readily imagine what would happen if several hundred hostile warriors got their hands on the excellent repeaters. They would wreak havoc from one end of Minnesota to the other, and beyond if they were so inclined. "How many Henrys are we talking about?" he asked.

Colonel Williams scowled. "That's where we're in the dark, I'm afraid. Fire Thunder wasn't specific. From what he told the Winnebago, our best guess is only two dozen or so."

"But you can see our dilemma," Captain Beckworth said. "Unless we cork the flow before it becomes a flood, no white this side of perdition will be safe."

Fargo was tempted to point out that the whites had brought it down on themselves by forcing the Indians off all the good land onto overcrowded reservations, where the tribes were required to give up the ways of their ancestors and adopt the strange customs of their conquerors. The Indians had been cheated, lied to, and outright abused. Small wonder that a war faction now craved vengeance.

"So even if you don't think talking to the Santees about honoring their end of the treaty will do any good," Beckworth said, "maybe you'll see fit to check into the gun-trafficking operation."

"I'll nose around and see what I can come up with," Fargo offered, and rose.

The officers did likewise, Colonel Williams saying, "What I can't figure out is who would be insane enough to arm the Sioux? It has to be someone with no scruples whatsoever." He offered his hand. "Until we meet again, kindly keep all this under your hat. We don't want word to get out and cause a panic."

Fargo made for the entrance, Beckworth falling into step beside him.

"We contacted the company that manufactures the Henrys, but they have no record of any large shipments being sent to Minnesota. We also contacted Washington, but they haven't replied yet." Beckworth grew sarcastic. "I guess they're assessing the situation before they commit themselves."

"How many Sioux villages are in the area at this time of year?" Fargo probed.

"Several, but the only one I can pinpoint for certain is up near Leech Lake. That's where one of their most respected leaders, Red Wing, spends most of the spring and summer every year."

Fargo was mildly surprised to find that Wagon Annie was gone. The post was back to normal. The wagon she had brought in was being unloaded. Fargo and the officer crossed the compound to the hitch rail where the Ovaro was tied.

"I can't thank you enough for coming, Skye," Beckworth said earnestly. "I wouldn't have bothered you with this, except we had no one else to turn to. And given the stakes—"

"There's no need to apologize," Fargo said, clapping his friend on the shoulder. "What happens here will have an impact on everyone everywhere. So I have a personal stake."

Mounting, Fargo rode out through the main gate and turned north toward Minneapolis. The town had grown by leaps and bounds since he saw it last. Ramshackle dwellings and dirty tents had given way to frame buildings and more substantial structures. The streets were still as dusty, though, and the populace just as rowdy. Maybe more so.

Lumbermen and farmers made up the bulk of the inhabitants. The former were usually loud and boisterous, the latter went about their business calmly and quietly. Mixed in among them were the town's residents; store clerks, bank tellers, accountants, and the like, most conspicuous due to their pale skins and paltry builds.

As Fargo passed a saloon, the door was smashed open by a flying body. A man whose clothes were little better than rags landed on his elbows and knees in the dirt, blood trickling from his nose. Inside, someone warned, "And don't come back unless you can pay for your drinks!"

At a corner stood two painted ladies who had no qualms about displaying their wares in broad daylight. One winked and crooked a finger, but Fargo merely grinned and shook his head.

The North Star Saloon was a new establishment. It was also one of the biggest and grandest. The sun had not yet gone down, but the place was doing a bustling business. Three hitch rails were not enough to hold the horses of its customers. Fargo went on by to a stable down the street to bed the stallion for the night. His bedroll and his own Henry were left with the proprietor for safekeeping.

After slicking his hair with water from a horse trough and brushing days of accumulated dust off his buckskins, Fargo was ready to treat himself to a night he would remember for a long time to come. Hooking his thumbs into his gun belt, he sauntered out into the wide street.

From out of nowhere flashed a long leather lash. It snagged his forearm, jerking him around to face its owner, who stood with her feet firmly planted and fire in her eyes. "I thought so! I saw you go past the saloon!" Wagon Annie said. She flicked her wrist. The bullwhip loosened, then coiled toward her as if it were alive. "Let's see how you like a taste of your own medicine!"

Fargo did not have to ask what she had in mind. He hurtled forward, legs churning, covering half the distance before the whip sailed up and out. He tried to sidestep, but she had anticipated him and the lash wrapped around his left ankle. Her squeal of laughter showed how much she enjoyed dumping him onto his back.

Rolling, Fargo grabbed the whip as it slid off his leg. Wagon Annie tugged, but he held on, determined not to let her swing it again. Gaining his knees, Fargo sought to wrench her off balance, but she was a lot stronger than her shapely figure suggested. Clinging to the handle, she resisted his every effort.

"No man has ever taken my Precious from me!" Wagon Annie boasted. "Ever!"

Precious? Fargo looked down at the whip. *She called it Precious!* It was a common practice on the frontier for men to give pet names to their rifles and horses and mules, but this was the first time he had ever heard of anyone bestowing a name on a *bullwhip*.

The distraction cost him. Wagon Annie suddenly dug in her heels and threw her entire weight backward. Fargo sprawled onto his belly, losing his grip, and the whip snaked off across the ground. He scrambled after it, but he was not quick enough to catch hold.

Wagon Annie's arm arced. The lash crackled like a gunshot, then descended toward Fargo's head. He flung himself to the right just in time.

Heaving upright, Fargo lowered his shoulders and charged like a bull gone amok. He managed to cover six feet before the stinging rawhide wrapped around his ankle and upended him. The redhead uttered a taunting laugh.

"What's the matter, big man? Had too much to drink?"

It occurred to Fargo that Wagon Annie was not seriously trying to hurt him or she would have done so by now. No, she was playing with him, paying him back for the sock to her gut by making a fool of him in front of half the population of Minneapolis.

Or so it seemed. People were flocking from every which way, lured by the ruckus and a human scarecrow in overalls who apparently had nothing better to do and had appointed himself the town crier. He was hollering for one and all to come witness Wagon Annie's latest temper tantrum. For two bits Fargo would have shot him.

The redhead circled, keeping her distance. She stung his left arm as he rose, stung his thigh as he zigzagged, feinting left and going right. Fargo saw her glance at his ankle and guessed where she would aim her next swing. He was ready when the lash shot toward him. A high, vaulting spring carried him over it, and he closed in.

Wagon Annie backpedaled while trying to draw back her whip for another try. She succeeded.

Fargo outfoxed her. He pretended to repeat the same zigzag pattern, only now he feinted left and went right. The lash buzzed past his ear and he was in the clear with only six feet to cover. He leaped, his outflung arms wrapping around her waist, his greater weight bearing her to the street.

If he thought that pinning her would end their clash, he thought wrong. Wagon Annie let go of the bullwhip, and flailed at his head and shoulders with fists as hard as anvils. She packed more muscle on her sinewy frame than most men, and she knew how to use it.

Wincing from the pain, Fargo tried to press his knees onto her arm. It was like trying to hold down a crazed bobcat. She fought fiercely, punching, jabbing, clawing, and scraping. Her long nails had the same effect as a bobcat's claws. One created a bloody furrow a finger's width from his eye.

Bellowing like a typical tavern brawler, Wagon Annie bucked and thrashed. Fargo did all he could to hold on, but it was like trying to ride a wild mustang for the very first time. Only without the aid of a halter and rope. He trapped her right arm under his leg, lunged to trap her left. She wriggled furiously, slipping free, and boxed both his ears.

Someone in the crowd thought that was hilarious. Residents ringed them, some urging Wagon Annie on, some shouting for Fargo to teach her a lesson, while others complained that they were making an indecent spectacle of themselves and demanded they quit behaving like children.

Annie unexpectedly flipped to the left, dumping Fargo on his side. She was on him like a sidewinder, straddling his chest to pummel his unprotected head. His hat had long since fallen off, but that was the least of his worries. Raising both arms, he warded off her hammering fists, suffering a single glancing jab to the cheek.

Somehow or other Fargo hooked an arm around her waist, and they wound up rolling madly toward the onlookers, her thigh wedged between his legs. Annie's long red hair covered his face, blinding him. He had to release her to swat it aside, and she instantly skittered onto her hands and feet, gave a strange little hop, and kicked at his nose.

Fargo spared himself by flinging his body to the rear. She pressed her attack, delivering a flurry of kicks to prevent him from getting to his feet. Her strategy worked until she kicked too hard, overextending herself. He snared her foot, twisted, and brought her tumbling down.

Unwinding like a steel spring, Fargo pounced. He landed on top of her—his chest mashing her ample bosom, his nose practically touching hers—and seized her wrists. She had plenty of fight left in her. He braced for the worst.

"Rip him apart, gal!" a partisan hollered.

Wagon Annie unaccountably stopped struggling. A smirk creased her luscious lips, and she did the last thing in the world Fargo would ever expect her to do. She kissed him full on the mouth.

"Damn, but you're a scrapper! You're the only man who's ever held his own against me except for Buffalo Charley, and the Blackfeet made wolf meat of him a few years back."

Fargo was too stunned by the kiss to respond. One moment the hellcat was trying to tear his eyes out, the next she was tracing her tongue across his mouth. Her lips had tasted every bit as delicious as they looked. He became aware of her earthy scent combined with a minty fragrance.

Covered with grime as she was from their struggle, her buckskins rumpled, her hair disheveled, she was undeniably one of the most lovely women he had ever met. His groin twitched.

"I knew you were my kind of man when you punched me," Annie continued merrily. "There ain't another coon in Minnesota with gumption enough to do that."

Words failed Fargo. Here he'd figured she would tear into him like a berserk mountain lion, yet she gave him compliments.

Wagon Annie snickered. "What's the matter? Cat got your tongue, handsome? Don't be so frazzled. When I set my sights on a gent, I like to test his mettle first." She playfully winked, then whispered, "Count yourself lucky. Ain't very many who can brag of bedding me."

A shadow fell across them. Confused, Fargo glanced up, thinking that a local lawman had arrived.

It was Ethan Lee. "We meet again, friend." The gambler dipped his hat to Wagon Annie. "Ma'am."

"Where did you come from?" Fargo asked, making no attempt to pry himself off the redhead.

"I happened to be riding by and saw your antics." Lee's pause was masterful. "Has anyone ever mentioned that you have a mighty peculiar way of winning over women?"

3

The patrons of the North Star Saloon were in a friendly, festive mood. To show their gratitude for what one lumberjack described as the "best entertainment we've had around here since two spattin' doves took to rippin' each other's dress off awhile back," they plied Wagon Annie and Skye Fargo with drink after drink.

Fargo nursed his, often leaving half a glass unfinished before he picked up the next. Annie, he noticed, gulped each and every one as if they were water. Incredibly, after six shot glasses of whiskey, she was as steady and clear-eyed as she had been when they ambled inside. He had never met anyone who could hold liquor like she could.

The redhead caught his look and bent, her mouth brushing his ear, her warm breath tingling his skin. "The hard stuff never fuddles my head," she said. "Don't ask me why. It must have something to do with the way I'm made. I've been like this since I was knee high to a grasshopper."

Ethan Lee had tagged along and stood to one side, amused by the whole affair. He had ordered a rye when they came in, but he hardly took three sips the whole evening.

At last the customers drifted off. Fargo was nibbling on jerky sold by the barkeep, when what he really wanted was an inch-thick steak with a mountain of trimmings. He mentioned as much to the redhead.

"Why didn't you say so sooner?" Wagon Annie said. "I could use with some grub myself. There's a place down the street that serves until midnight. What do you say to moseying on over and gorging ourselves like a pair of hogs?"

Lee chortled. "You sure do have a colorful way with words, ma'am," he said politely. "I like the idea, though. What with having to fetch a doctor for that lumberman whose leg you busted, and taking care of my horse, I haven't had a bite to eat, either."

Annie was leaning on the counter, about to down another whiskey. "I don't recall inviting you, cardsharp." She rubbed against Fargo and delicately traced a fingernail along the outline of his jaw. "This here is the he-bear I aim to get acquainted with. Skye and me want to be alone after we leave here, don't we, handsome?"

The gambler set down his whiskey. "I know when I'm not wanted," he said. With a nod, he blended into the bedlam.

"You had no reason to be rude," Fargo criticized, putting his own glass next to Lee's. "He was only being friendly."

Annie was staring into the throng. "Think so? Tell me, how long have the two of you been acquainted?"

"We met today," Fargo admitted.

"Then, you don't know him very well, do you?" Annie placed her warm hand over his. "I didn't mean to ruffle your feathers, big man. But I'd watch myself around him if I were you. He's hiding something."

"What do you mean?"

Wagon Annie shrugged. "I can't rightly say, but I could see it in his eyes when he looked at you when your back was turned. Trust me. I can read men as if they were open books."

Fargo scanned the crowd but saw no sign of the gambler. He wondered if the redhead was right, or whether the whiskey was having an effect on her after all. "I'll keep it in mind," he said, doubting anything would ever come of it.

A commotion broke out near the entrance. Three men in uniforms were shouldering through the customers with no regard for anyone. In the lead stalked a living brick wall, a man wider than he was tall. His face gave the impression of being carved from marble, his expression permanently set in an attitude of smug arrogance.

"Speaking of books," Wagon Annie said, and she did not sound pleased, "here comes one I'd rather not read. Let's get going before I do something I'll regret."

Fargo had his arm snatched. She hustled him to the left to avoid the newcomers, but the brick wall spotted her and changed course, halting directly in their path. To Fargo's surprise, Annie's grip tightened, as if she were afraid. It was hard to conceive of her being scared of anyone. He scrutinized the brick wall and did not like what he saw.

The uniforms the trio wore were not Army issue. They were brown, not blue, with silver buttons and silver trim at the ends of the sleeves and the pants. The leader's also had silver epaulets on both shoulders, wide lapels decorated with silver swirls, and button-down cuffs. His buttonholes were embroidered with silver, and silver studs adorned his boots.

Fargo had never seen the like. It reminded him of a character he had once seen in a theatrical production. Without thinking, he quipped, "Lost your army, General?" and right away knew he had said the wrong thing. The man glowered like a grizzly about to charge.

Wagon Annie laughed much longer and louder than the comment called for. Raising a hand to the bullwhip coiled over her right shoulder, she said with biting contempt, "This is no general, Skye. This here is Major Mortimer Gatz of the Minnesota Militia. He spruced up his uniform just so he can strut around like a fancy peacock."

Major Gatz fixed a baleful gaze on the redhead. "Woman," he said in greeting, contriving to make that single word ring with loathing and spite, "I didn't come here looking for more trouble from the likes of you."

"Then, get the hell out of our way," Wagon Annie bristled.

"After I've talked to your friend," Gatz countered, pivoting. "You are Skye Fargo, I presume?"

"I am," Fargo confirmed, hiding his instinctive dislike for the popinjay.

"Excellent. I visited Colonel Williams a short while ago, and he told me about you. Allow me to be one of the first to wish you success in your venture, and to offer the services of my company if you should require them. We're all seasoned Indian fighters."

Her brow knitting, Wagon Annie glanced around. "What is he talking about, handsome?"

The popinjay answered first. "Do you mean to tell me there is something you *don't* know? Mr. Fargo is going to track down the vermin who have been selling repeaters to the Santees before they wipe the whole lot of us out."

Everyone within earshot stopped whatever they were doing and turned.

"What was that about repeaters?" one asked.

"In the hands of the stinkin' Sioux?" chimed in another.

It took all of Fargo's self-control for him not to flatten the major. Not only had the fool revealed information the Army wanted kept secret, but now, within a day or two, everyone in the territory would know that he was on the trail of the gun traffickers, *including the gun traffickers.*

Gatz clasped his ham-size hands behind his broad back and regarded his audience haughtily. "You heard correctly, citizens. Our illustrious state faces a danger of supreme magnitude. We all know how resentful the Santees have become of late, and how they are just itching for an excuse to start taking scalps. Think of the destruction they can wreak armed with the latest rifles!"

More and more patrons were crowding around to hear, most from the bar. Fargo took a step, gripped the major by the elbow, and steered him to the now-empty counter. "Are you loco?" he snapped. "Keep that up, and you'll have a bloodbath on your hands! The Sioux aren't the only ones itching for war."

36

The major jerked his arm loose and smoothed his sleeve. "So? You make it sound as if exterminating those filthy savages would be a tragedy." He sniffed, then declared, "Don't tell me you're one of those squeamish Indian lovers? If you knew them like I do, you'd hate them as much as me."

Fargo blundered. He was so incensed that he blurted, "I've lived with the Dakotas, mister."

Mortimer Gatz stiffened. "Oh, really?" he growled, and raked Fargo from head to toe with a withering look. "I've heard of men like you, traitors to your own kind, but I've never had the misfortune to meet one face-to-face." He sneered. "Tell me, did you have your own squaw? Did she keep your bed warm at night, and bear you a pack of vicious little half-breeds?"

Fargo could not help himself. His right first exploded against the major's jaw, tottering Gatz backward. The militiaman collided with a chair and table. All three crashed to the floor in a tangle of human and wooden legs.

Just like that, the North Star Saloon became as quiet as a tomb. All eyes were on Fargo and Gatz as the latter shoved the chair aside and slowly rose. Gatz was livid. He shrugged off the help of the two soldiers who rushed to his assistance, adjusted his coat, and snarled, "You just made the biggest mistake of your life, Skye Fargo. I'm not someone who takes insults lightly. This doesn't end here."

With that, Major Gatz stormed from the premises, his underlings in tow. Murmuring broke out as the bartender came around the end of the bar to replace the furniture.

Fargo grew aware of someone standing at his elbow. He thought it would be Wagon Annie, but it was Ethan Lee, gun hand hooked in his red sash close to the pearl-handled Colt.

"You sure do have a knack for antagonizing folks," the man in black commented. "It's a good thing you aren't going into politics."

Fargo searched for Annie, but she was nowhere to be

seen. Exasperated, he went out. The sun had set and darkness sheathed Minneapolis. From another saloon across the street issued the tinny music of a piano. He inhaled the crisp air and smelled wood smoke. It was the supper hour for the town's families.

As he turned to leave, Fargo saw several grubby men glaring at him through the large front window. Public sentiment toward the Indians being what it was, he'd have to watch his back every minute of every day from then on.

Somewhere along the line, Fargo had lost his appetite. The notion of that thick steak no longer appealed to him. He decided to find a hotel and take a room. It would be the first time in weeks he had slept in a bed.

By asking several people, Fargo learned of a place a few blocks away that would do him just fine. He was almost abreast of an alley when he heard low voices, speaking angrily. One was a woman's. Slowing, he discovered Wagon Annie and a tall man in an expensive set of clothes framed in the alley mouth. She had her back to him, and the man was intent on her.

"—Told you once, I've told you a million times," the redhead was saying. "The answer is still no."

"Not even for a thousand dollars more?" the tall man said. "Think of it. You could buy yourself some dresses and head east to the States. Live like a real lady for a while."

Wagon Annie braced her hands on her hips. "Why in tarnation would I want to do that? I'm happy the way I am, Wallace. And I'm keeping my freight line no matter how much money you offer." She went to leave, but Wallace grabbed her wrist.

"Damn it all, Annie, be reasonable. Freighting is no fit business for a woman. And you're on your own now that your two drivers have quit."

"Were chased off, you mean, by you and your bullies," Annie replied, prying at his fingers. "Don't think I don't know what you're up to. You're not offering to buy me out

38

for my own good. You want to be the only freighter in the territory so you can double, even triple, your profits."

Wallace refused to remove his hand. "What's wrong with that?" he said. "Profits grease the wheels of enterprise, my dear. I'm a businessman, just like Ferguson at the general store and Howard at the millinery."

"The difference," Annie said harshly while trying harder to loosen his grip, "is that Ferguson and Howard are honest men, and you're not. If you had a monopoly, you'd gouge your customers for every cent you could wring out of them." She tugged, then rasped, "Let go of me, damn you!"

An oily smile creased Wallace's ferret face. "Not until you agree to my proposal."

Fargo had observed long enough. Striding into the open, he declared, "I'd do as she wants if I were you, mister."

Wallace straightened and lowered his arm. His hand began to drift under the immaculate coat he wore. "Who asked you to butt in, stranger? This is strictly between Miss Standley and myself."

To Fargo's surprise, Wagon Annie said curtly, "That's right, Skye. I don't need looking after. Do me a favor and stay away from me, you hear?"

The revelation stopped Wallace's hand. "You know this man?" he asked.

"He's working for the Army," the redhead divulged. "The Santees have gotten their hands on some repeating rifles. He's supposed to find out who gave them the guns."

"Do tell," Wallace said, and stepped into the street, where the glow from a lantern in a window above highlighted his rodent-like profile. "I daresay you have your work cut out for you, sir. The Sioux will not take kindly to your meddling." He held out his hand. "Forgive me for being so defensive. I'm Edward Wallace, owner of Wallace Freighting."

The man's shake was as limp as a wet towel. "No harm done," Fargo said lamely.

"I take it you've heard of me?"

"Who hasn't?" Fargo said, being perfectly truthful. The Wallace freighting firm was a mammoth concern that operated in Minnesota and three other states. At the rate it was growing, Wallace Freighting promised to be the largest in the whole country before the decade was out.

"I sincerely hope you can stop the Santees from causing any trouble," Wallace said. "It would be bad for business. War always is. Schedules are disrupted. Freight doesn't get through. Merchandise is lost. It's my worst nightmare come true."

No mention, Fargo noted, of the many deaths that would result. No mention of the innocents who would suffer. All that mattered to Wallace was the business end. Profit and loss. The ledger was more important than the lives.

"I'll keep my ears to the ground, as it were," Wallace proposed. "A man in my position often hears things that others do not. Anything of substance will be relayed to you."

"I'm obliged," Fargo said. The man bowed in courtly fashion to Annie, then walked off whistling softly. Annie started to depart in the other direction. "Hold on," Fargo said. "We need to talk."

She halted, but she would not face him. "About what?"

"Why did you run off? What have I done that made you so upset?"

Wagon Annie's shoulders slumped. "You would never understand, handsome. Let's just say that the two of us getting together ain't in the cards, and let it go at that." She ran to the next corner, her long red tresses whipping in the stiff breeze. At the last moment, she glanced sadly over her shoulder.

Now, what in the world had that been all about? Fargo mused. She was acting as if she were the one who had something to hide, not Ethan Lee. Shaking his head, he trudged on. The situation was more confusing by the moment.

Ahead was the last turn before the hotel. Since the night

was moonless and none of the adjacent buildings had lights in them, the intersection was as murky as the bottom of a well. Fargo was walking close to the structures on the right-hand side. The street was momentarily deserted except for a stray dog that gave him a wide birth.

Fargo passed a cabin. Between it and the next frame building lay an inky patch of grass. Without warning, a shadow detached itself from the blackness and rammed into his shins, bowling him over. He slammed onto his spine, the world blurring around him. But he had the presence of mind to roll, and as he did, a heavy boot brushed his ear.

"Grab him, damn it!" someone hissed.

More shadows pounced. Fargo's head cleared, but not in time to prevent two brawny forms from grasping him on either side and hauling him onto the grass.

"Now, beat him senseless," the same man directed.

A third figure materialized in front of Fargo and drew back a fist. In the darkness the gleam of his grim was like a miniature quarter moon. It gave Fargo an ideal spot to aim at as he levered his legs upward, using the men who were holding him for support. His foot smashed into the smirker's mouth, and the man staggered.

"Hold him, you fools!"

Fargo shifted to the right, then to the left. The men who had seized him held on tight, but they were powerless to stop him from twisting and kicking the one on the left in the knee. There was a sharp pop. The man howled and let go, his stricken leg buckling.

"Can't you people do anything right?" demanded the skulker by the cabin.

A right cross to the jaw of the shadow still holding him sufficed to free Fargo, and he spun to go after the brains behind the attack. He took a long bound, only to be intercepted by a pair of husky bruisers who waded into him with their own fists flying.

Fargo blocked a jab, slipped a hook, and sidestepped an uppercut. A left caught him on the chin, but not hard enough to do any damage. In retaliation he drove his right fist into the stomach of the man responsible. The blow would have dropped most men, but this one was wearing a thick jacket or coat.

"Hurry up before someone comes by!" the mastermind said. Whoever he was, he was trying to disguise his voice by lowering it drastically and adopting a gravel tone.

Four men now had Fargo hemmed in, and they had learned from their mistakes. Rather than come at him a few at a time, they converged in concert, raining blows without letup. Fargo countered half, if that. Iron knuckles pounded his temples, his face, his shoulders. His left eyebrow split. His own blood blinded him. Ever so slowly, he weakened.

The inevitable occurred. Fargo was battered to his knees. His skull rang like a bell, and he could barely see straight. The men who had pummeled him had him at their mercy, but, strangely, they stepped back instead of pressing their advantage.

Another man advanced. Like the others, he was as black as pitch. But even in Fargo's groggy state, there was no mistaking the man's broad, stout build. He resembled a brick wall, a living brick wall.

"I told you that I do not take insults lightly," Major Mortimer Gatz said, bending until his stern features loomed above Fargo's. "Army or no Army, you have until tomorrow noon to clear out of the territory. If you don't, I'll have you pounded to a pulp every time you turn around."

Fargo's fury lent him the strength to spit out, "Save your breath, coward! I'm not going anywhere until the job is done."

Gatz's facial muscles twitched as if he were having a fit. "You dare call *me* yellow?" He lashed out, racking Fargo with severe agony. "Me? The man who formed the Minnesota Militia? Me? The man who took a ragtag bunch of misfits and turned them into a superior fighting force?" Again he struck.

Fargo was fading fast. He yearned to stay conscious long

enough to land one solid hit. Unfortunately, Gatz's features kept blinking out like a signal lantern. "Only a coward lets others do his dirty work," he was able to croak.

It was Fargo's intention to make Gatz so mad that the officer would lean even closer. But the insult only elicited a sneer.

"You're a bigger fool than I imagined. Very well, mister. The next time I will deal with you myself."

One of the soldiers snickered. "What a jackass, sir! I guess he's never seen you lift two anvils at once."

Mortimer Gatz stepped back into the shadows. "Finish him, Private Jenkins. But be careful. We don't want him to die or his friend, Captain Beckworth, might launch an investigation."

"My pleasure, sir." Jenkins moved forward to deliver the final punch. "Just kneel there a moment longer, and it will all be over," he said.

It was not in Fargo's nature to go meekly to the slaughter. He was a wolf, not a lamb. He'd once heard a parson state that it was always better to turn the other cheek when threatened with violence. Easy for the parson to say, when the Bible thumper was safe on a podium, surrounded by his peace-loving flock.

But what was a man to do when unfriendly Kiowas thirsted for his blood? When a war party of Blackfeet had him trapped and would surely separate him from his hair if he did not fight back? When outlaws and cutthroats and killers of every stripe came at him with a dirk, a knife or a gun? Was he supposed to turn the other cheek then? Because if he did, he was as good as dead, and Fargo liked living too much to give up the ghost without a struggle.

So now, as Private Jenkins reared above him and raised a stony fist, Fargo did what he would always do in similar situations. Girding his legs, he threw all the reserves he had left into a punch to Jenkins's stomach, a punch that whooshed the breath from the private's lungs and sent him weaving off as if drunk, hands clasped over his gut.

"Must I do everything myself?" Major Gatz said, disgusted. He moved in, adopting a boxing stance.

Fargo tried to defend himself. He truly did. But he was next to helpless to ward off the punishment he took. Dimly, he felt himself sag onto his side and heard Gatz's grating laugh.

"Remember, mister, this is just a taste of things to come. Be gone by noon tomorrow, or you'll be in for more of the same. Savvy?"

Fargo could not have answered if his life depended on it. Thankfully, a few seconds later, the darkness claimed his mind as well as his surroundings.

4

The first sensation Skye Fargo grew aware of was pain. Lots and lots of it. He blinked awake and regretted being so rash. Sunlight streaming in a nearby window fell full on his face, hurting his eyes terribly, adding to the misery he already felt. "Damn," he muttered absently.

"Is that you, stranger? Have you rejoined the world of the living?"

Fargo raised his head to find out where he was. Somehow or other he had wound up in a musty bed in a starkly furnished room with log walls. The scent of lavender and pink curtains were surefire signs that the occupant of the room must be female. A quilt covered him to the chin. Lifting the edge, he discovered he was buck naked.

"Damn," he said again.

Through a doorway came a slender blond woman in a light blue dress that had seen a lot of wear and tear. "You are awake," she said happily. "Land sakes, you had me worried. I was beginning to think I'd have to fetch the doctor, and he doesn't come cheap." She sat on the edge of the bed, then pressed a warm palm to his brow. "No fever. That's always a good sign."

Fargo had to swallow twice before his vocal cords would work. "Where am I? And who are you?"

"You're in the cabin I rent on Hennepin Street. I found you in front of it last night when I came home from work," the blond explained.

Fargo recalled that the militiamen had dragged him

into the small front yard of a cabin when they jumped him.

"It was so dark, I might not have noticed you at all if you hadn't groaned as I was opening the door," the woman went on. "I had a terrible time toting you inside, as big and heavy as you are." She paused. "I'm Cassie Abernathy, by the way. Most folks just call me Cass."

"I'm in your debt," Fargo said, his voice like sandpaper grating on metal. "And I'd be ever more in your debt if I could have something to drink."

"Of course. Right away."

Cass bustled out, and Fargo sank onto the pillow. A red haze spawned by raw rage shimmered before his eyes as he thought again of the attack, and Major Gatz's ultimatum. With a toss of his head, he got a grip on himself and willed his body to relax. Gatz was going to pay for what he had done, and pay dearly.

The blond returned bearing a glass filled with water. "I'm sorry," she said. "This is the best I can do. I can't afford liquor. Or milk, generally."

That made twice she had hinted a lack of money. Fargo thanked her and sipped, savoring the relief it brought his throat. She had an accent that he could not quite place. New England, he suspected. "Do you live here alone?" he asked.

"Except for Shawn," Cass said, her face brightening. "Usually, I keep him in here with me, but since I slept on the couch last night, I pushed his crib into the other room."

"You have a baby?"

"Two months old. Let me show him to you." Cass hurried out and was back in no time with an infant swaddled in a blanket that had to be the newest article in the cabin. The child was sleeping, and she gently peeled back the blanket so Fargo could see the child's angelic countenance. "Isn't he wonderful?" she breathed, smiling in rapture.

"Who's the lucky father?" Fargo inquired, wondering if perhaps the man would show up and become incensed at finding him in their bed.

Cass's smile evaporated like dew under a hot sun. Her happiness gave way to the most abject sorrow, and for a moment it appeared she would burst into tears. Biting her lower lip, she coughed lightly, then said, "Simon, my husband. He was killed about a month ago when a tree fell on him." She bit her lip again. "He was a lumberjack, you see. We came all the way from Maine about a year ago."

Insight dawned, and Fargo understood her predicament. They were a young couple who had heard about all the money to be made in the booming timber trade in Minnesota. Like hundreds of other lumbermen, her husband had figured his prospects would be better there than in Maine, where the industry was in a slump. So they had packed up their meager belongings and traveled to Minneapolis.

It must have come as a shock for them to learn that while there was plenty of work to be found, the wages were so low that the average lumberjack had to put in long, grueling hours just to make ends meet. Probably, the husband had elected to stay on anyway in the hope of becoming a crew foreman eventually, and doubling his pay.

No one, though, could afford to take that sort of work for granted. It was a dangerous profession. There were hundreds of ways to die, and hundreds of timbermen did, each and every year. They were crushed by felled trees that did not fall exactly as planned, as Simon Abernathy must have been. Or they would fall themselves when working as high climbers.

"I'm sorry," Fargo said, and meant it. Cassie had to be an awfully kind, trusting woman to take a perfect stranger into her house.

She held her baby closer to her bosom. "I'll get over it soon enough," she lied. "I have to, for Shawn's sake."

"It must be a challenge for you to get by," Fargo mentioned. Single women were often hard-pressed to keep food on the table. Decent jobs were scarce, and those that could be had usually paid wages lower than a man would receive for the same work. Many, in desperation, wound up in saloons.

The blond nodded, her sorrow deepening. "I won't deny that it is. I've been trying to secure work so I can save enough to go back to Maine. But no one is hiring at the moment." She swallowed hard. "Although Mr. Prine has offered me a position."

The name meant nothing to Fargo. He finished the water, and she took the glass. "What did you do with my things?"

Cass pointed at the floor. "I folded your shirt and pants and put them under the bed along with your pistol and that knife you carry in your boot." Her mouth curled in a lopsided grin. "If it's not rude of me to want to know, who are you?"

Only then did Fargo realize he had neglected to tell her his name. He did, and as she turned to go, he lightly touched her wrist. "I can't thank you enough for what you've done, Mrs. Abernathy. If there is any way I can repay you, let me know."

Cass started at the contact, then said warmly, "There's no need. What kind of person would I be if I let someone suffer on the cold ground all night?" She closed the door as she went out.

Throwing off the quilt, Fargo swung his legs over the side of the bed and sat up. The cabin had a plank floor that creaked as he padded to a small mirror to take stock. He had a gash over his left eyebrow and a welt on his temple, as well as more bruises than he cared to count. Additional ones dotted his shoulders and upper arms. "You'll get yours, Gatz," he said softly.

His belongings were right where Cass had said they would be. Dressing quickly, Fargo attached the slender sheath that held his Arkansas toothpick to his right ankle, then pulled on his boots. The gun belt went around his waist. Last, he donned his hat.

He hesitated before reaching into his pocket. If any of the money he had won in Denver was gone, it would lower his estimation of Cassie considerably. He would walk out without another word to her. His fingers dipped—and found the wad of bills, all three hundred and forty-two dollars. She must have felt the money when she folded his pants, must have known it was there, yet, as poor was she was, she had not helped herself to any of it. "I'll be damned," he said.

Loud pounding suddenly sounded in the other room. The infant squalled, and Cassie called out, "Just a moment, please. I'll be right there."

Fargo drifted to the bedroom door and opened it a crack. She was picking the baby up out of a crib and trying to comfort him. Just as the infant quieted, someone outside pounded on the front door again. Shawn bawled, and he was still crying when Cassie reached the front door to admit her visitor.

A portly man with greasy hair and a bowler hat brushed by the widow without so much as a how-do-you-do? He regarded the few pieces of furniture and the shabby state of the room with disdain. Twirling a cane that had an ivory knob at the end, he gave the baby the same look he had given the cabin. "Can't you shut him up, Mrs. Abernathy? How are we to conduct business with him caterwauling like that?"

"I'm sorry," Cass said, rocking the infant, "but you scared him by knocking so loud. The next time, rap lightly, will you?"

"If there is a next time," her visitor declared. "That depends on your decision. Have you made up your mind?"

Cass moved to the crib and carefully deposited Shawn. Only Fargo could see her face. Only he saw the deep sadness and weariness that made her eyes glisten. "I'm still thinking about your offer, Mr. Prine."

Prine puffed in irritation "Really, my dear. I don't see what there is to think about. You're practically destitute. Without money, what will become of your child? How can you possibly get by?"

Cassie took a breath, dabbed at the corners of her eyes, and swung around. "It's not a decision that can be made lightly. I've never even been in a saloon, let alone worked in one. The very idea frightens me."

Fargo's eyes narrowed. Had he heard correctly?

"Come now," Prine huffed, casually moving toward her. "You're a grown woman. You have nothing to fear."

"But the stories I've heard—" Cass said.

Her greasy visitor cut her off with a wave of a pudgy hand. "Oh, honestly, Mrs. Abernathy. If all the tales told about the women who work in saloons were true, no woman would be caught dead in one. The fact that so many do work in them is proof that it can't be as bad as you imagine." Prine halted and leaned on his cane.

"Maybe so," Cass responded, "but I still don't know if it's right. My mother would roll over in her grave, God rest her soul."

"Your mother?" Prine snorted. "Maybe I was mistaken about you. I took you to be more mature than you are, more wise in the ways of the world." He sidled a few inches closer. "Sure, some of the girls who work for me become intimate with customers on occasion, but that's not to say that all of them do. The choice is strictly yours. Your job would be to entertain, to keep the men happy, to see that they drink as much as their billfolds will allow."

Cass had a hand on her baby, rubbing Shawn's belly. "I doubt I'd be very good at it. That's why I haven't gotten back to you."

Fargo opened the bedroom door a bit farther. He had an idea what was going to happen next, and he wanted to be ready.

"Nonsense, my dear," Prine said suavely, favoring her with a wolfish appraisal of her attractive body. "You sell yourself short. Why, half the women who work for me are not nearly as pretty as you are." He sidled nearer still, so close that his protruding stomach brushed her hip.

Cass backed up, but had nowhere to go. She was trapped

between the crib and the cabin wall. "Please, Mr. Prine. You're crowding me. Why don't you take a seat, and I'll make you some tea?"

"I never touch the stuff. Bad for the health," Prine joked, and was disappointed when she did not laugh. Annoyed, he tapped his foot, saying, "What has gotten into you? Here I thought I was doing you a favor."

"I know, but—" Cass tried to respond.

Prine was not listening. He was too full of himself. "I'm a highly respected businessman, Mrs. Abernathy. Several councilmen are personal friends of mine. When I heard from one of them that you had shown up at his place asking for work, I took it on myself to come to your aid. Out of the goodness of my own heart, I offered you a position that a dozen other women would sell their souls to have." Prine inched forward so that he had Cassie pinned.

"Please," Cass repeated. "Step back or I'll scream."

"I wouldn't, if I were you," Prine advised, smacking the crib with his cane. "Think of your baby."

"Oh, God!" Cassie said.

Fargo was through the doorway and on top of them before either were aware of him. He seized Prine by the scruff of the neck, pivoted, and shoved. The saloon owner crashed into the couch, almost upending it. His hat fell to the floor. With remarkable agility for someone so overweight, he whirled and raised his cane.

"Who the hell are you?"

Angling to a spot between Prine and the front door, Fargo said, "Apologize to the lady, then get your slimy carcass out of here."

Prine hefted his walnut cane. "And what if I don't, bastard? What are you going to do about it?"

Fargo never hesitated. His fists balled, he sprang. The ivory knob whistled at his head, but he ducked. His right fist sank to the wrist on Prine's flabby stomach, his left smashed an ear so that blood flew. His fury was so great that he barely heard Cassie's cry.

"Skye, don't! He's not worth it!"

The cane clipped Fargo on the shoulder. Tearing it from Prine's grasp, he rammed the ivory knob into Prine's groin. The saloon owner squeaked like a mouse, stumbled a few feet, covered himself, and collapsed onto his knees. Fargo slowly drew his Colt.

"No!" Prine blubbered.

Cassie dashed over. "You wouldn't!" she said, her eyes pleading. "Not here! Not with the baby in the room!"

Brushing her aside, Fargo extended the pistol, touched the barrel to Prine's temple, and slowly cocked the hammer. Prine wailed just as the baby had done and bowed his forehead to the floor, tears streaming over his fleshy jowls.

"Don't, mister! For the love of God! I'll leave and never come back! You have my word!"

For several seconds Fargo held the revolver steady. Then he eased the hammer down and he twirled the Colt into his holster with a flourish. "Scum like you should be tarred and feathered." Stooping, he grasped Prine by the shoulders, heaved him to his feet, and flung him at the front door.

Prine was not able to stay erect. His shoulder smashed into it with a resounding thud. Crying out, he rose unsteadily, fumbling at the latch. "What about my hat and my cane?" he bleated.

Fargo still held the latter in his left hand. Savagely, he broke it across his knee and cast the two pieces at the saloon owner's feet. "Buy yourself another one."

Cassie retrieved the bowler hat. Prine snatched it and was out the door, racing toward the street as if he had wings on his feet. She watched him go. Then she faced Fargo, her eyes glistening once more, only this time for an entirely different reason. "Thank you," she whispered.

Fargo felt uncomfortable under her frank stare. "I have to go now," he said. "I'll check back later to make sure that buzzard has kept his word."

"I'd be honored if you would let me treat you to supper,"

Cass said anxiously. "I'm not the best cook in the world, but my Simon claimed I'm better than most."

Fargo opened his mouth to say no. As much as he would have liked to, he needed to head out while the day was still young. Colonel Williams had told him he would find the Sioux village near Leech Lake, and it would take him days to get there.

"Please," Cassie said. "I could use the company. I hardly ever get visitors, and it would be nice to have someone to talk to." She folded her hands in entreaty. "Besides, in another few hours it will be suppertime anyway."

"What time is it?" Fargo asked in surprise. A clock on a mantel over the fireplace informed him that it was half past four. Evidently, he had been unconscious most of the day. It changed everything. "I have to run to Fort Snelling first."

Cassie was elated. "No problem. It will give me time to make a proper meal." She glanced at her pantry and frowned. "Just don't expect anything lavish. Groceries are hard to come by."

"Whatever you cook will be fine," Fargo assured her. Leaving, he paused to survey the street. No militiamen were in sight. Mortimer Gatz would take it for granted that he had been scared off, which was a big mistake on the major's part.

On the way to the stable Fargo stopped at a general store. The proprietor gawked when he began piling item after item on the counter. Coffee, salt, cheese, baking soda, sugar, vinegar, spices, a pot and pans, even strips of bacon and a ham that had been hanging from the ceiling. A pair of dresses that appeared to be Cassie's size were added to the growing pile. Last of all he selected a bright green infant's rattle.

"A married man, I see," the proprietor said as Fargo prepared to pay.

"Not in this life," Fargo quipped. He scribbled a note for Cassie that read, "*I always pay my debts*," and gave directions to her cabin. "See that all this is delivered within half an hour."

The proprietor peered over the top of his spectacles at the mountains of merchandise. "That soon? It will take me at least that long to load it on the wagon."

"Half an hour," Fargo insisted, peeling off five extra dollars.

"You can count on me, sir!"

Next stop, Fargo visited a butcher and instructed the man to deliver five pounds of fresh beef. He was a block from the stable when he saw a millinery on the second floor of a building that also housed a shoemaker. A bell above the door chimed noisily when he opened it, drawing the attention of three matrons who were browsing by the shelves.

A gray-haired man behind the counter squinted at him in disapproval. "I daresay you have the wrong establishment, sir. The tobacco shop is in the next building over."

Fargo stalked to a table piled high with boxes and rummaged through them. There were more styles than he had counted on. Some with lace. Some with ribbons. "I need a hat for a friend," he said as the owner came over.

"Ah. Indeed. Do you happen to know her size?" the man asked.

Fargo was stumped. Women's sizes were not the same as for men. He walked toward the matrons, who shrank back as if in fear of losing their womanly virtue. One had a head the size of a watermelon, the other was a dainty snip of a thing, but the third was about the same height and weight as Cassie. "My friend is her size," he told the owner, and doffed his hat. "Ma'am, I would be grateful if you would help me pick the kind of bonnet that you would wear."

The matron he had chosen was suddenly all smiles. Preening for the benefit of her companions, she allowed Fargo to guide her to the table, where she hemmed and hawed until Fargo was nearly ready to scream. At last she narrowed her choice to one. Fargo offered extra money to the milliner to have it delivered.

"That won't be necessary, young man," the owner said. "I will personally take it at no additional charge."

Fargo remembered the conversation he had overheard between Wagon Annie and Edward Wallace. "Your name wouldn't be Howard by any chance, would it?"

The man blinked. "Yes, it is. Why? Have we met before?"

"No," Fargo said, turning. "It's just that you're one of the last of a dying breed."

"And what breed might that be, sir?"

"You're an honest man."

Howard's puzzled gaze followed Fargo out the door and partway down the outside stairs. At the bottom he bent his steps to the stable and was crossing the threshold when a familiar voice brought him up short.

"At last! I was beginning to think we would miss each other!"

Captain Jim Beckworth had been lounging against a stall, talking to the liveryman. "I spent most of the day hunting for you," he said as he came over. "I took a chance that you hadn't left yet, and checked all the stables in town for a horse like yours."

"Has something happened?" Fargo asked.

Beckworth motioned toward a corner, saying quietly, "It's not common knowledge yet, but a handful of Santees armed with repeaters attacked a wood detail out of Fort Ripley. One soldier was wounded and six horses were stolen."

Fort Ripley, as Fargo recollected, was north of Minneapolis, the closest post to Leech Lake.

"I'm leading a patrol there at dawn, and I thought you might want to tag along. A company of Minnesota Militia will accompany us, led by their commander, Major Mortimer Gatz. I don't like the man, myself. He's a bigot and a blowhard. But Colonel Williams is a stickler for cooperating with the locals."

"Count me in," Fargo said, inwardly smiling at the ironic

whims of fate. He had been on his way to Fort Snelling to learn where Gatz was headquartered, and now he need not bother.

"Good. I knew I could." Beckworth took a pocket watch out. "I'd like to stay and sling the bull, but I have to be back at the post before dark. Until tomorrow."

Fargo waved as the officer mounted and departed. Since he had time to kill, he gave the Ovaro a rubdown and fed the stallion some oats by hand. Evening had fallen when he reached the Abernathy cabin and knocked twice. He hoped that Cassie would not make too much of what he had done. A thank-you would do.

Then the door flew open. The widow flung her arms around him, molded her body to him, and smothered his mouth with her own.

5

Skye Fargo stood flat-footed with amazement as the woman he had taken to be as shy as a mouse covered his lips and cheeks with hot, passionate kisses. When she drew back, she was flushed and breathing hard. She pulled him inside, giggling like a girl of ten or twelve.

"Whatever got into you? You did not have to do all this!" Cassie exclaimed, gesturing at the merchandise, food, and clothes that had arrived in his absence. "There's enough to feed us for a month of Sundays! And those dresses! They're so darling! How did you know I would like them?"

She was bubbling like a stream and would have gushed on in her excitement had Fargo not covered her mouth with his hand and said, "Calm down before you pop your buttons. Consider it my way of thanking you."

"Oh, Skye! You shouldn't have!" Cass said, her expression putting the lie to her statement. "Tomorrow I'll dress up, and we can take little Shawn for a stroll down by the river. Afterward, I'll fix any kind of meal you want. Name your favorite."

"Cassie—" Fargo said.

"I haven't been this happy since before Simon died," she raved on, her hands held to her throat. "For the first time in weeks, I don't need to worry about how I'll scrape up enough food to eat. And that bonnet! It's priceless!"

"Cassie, I—"

"Here. Take a look at Shawn." She guided him to the

crib, where the infant was playing with the rattle. "See that smile on his face? It's all thanks to you. You've brought some sunshine into our lives again." Cassie pressed against him, looping her arms around his neck. "I imagine Simon would roll over in his grave if he could see me being so forward, but I can't help how I feel."

Fargo had to stop her before she got even more carried away with herself. "Cassie, I'm leaving at first light. I doubt I'll be back again," he bluntly confessed.

"What?" She recoiled, conflicting emotions mirrored by her rippling features. "Oh! Goodness gracious! I see! And here I am making a spectacle of myself. I'm so sorry." She snapped her hands down as if she had touched burning embers.

"I have a job to do for the Army," Fargo explained, but it did no good. The damage had been done. The sorrow that had ruled her for so long reasserted itself. She headed for the stove, fiddling with her hair even though every strand was in its proper place.

"Please forgive me, Skye. I don't know what came over me." Cassie checked the contents of a pot. "Well, that's not quite true. I do know. For a little while there I felt alive again. It was wonderful."

The infant dropped the rattle, then twisted his head from side to side as if searching for it.

Fargo did not have much experience with babies. He always felt a sense of wonder around them. They were so frail, so vulnerable, so dependent on others to survive. It was a miracle that any did on the frontier, where life was so harsh and the weak so often fell victim to the merciless demands of wilderness existence.

He picked up the rattle and gingerly placed the handle in Shawn's little hands. The infant's tiny pale fingers brushed his big bronzed ones, affording a stark contrast. He smiled, and so did the baby.

Cassie was taking silverware to the small table. "I suppose I should look at the bright side," she commented.

"Now we'll get by until I get a job. And once I've saved enough, we can head back to Maine. All my relatives are there, and so are Simon's. They'll help us get on our feet."

"You'll do fine," Fargo predicted. He could tell she was still embarrassed so he changed the subject, making small talk until supper was ready. And what a supper it was. She had fixed roast beef and ham and mashed potatoes with gravy, as well as all the fixings. He gorged himself to show his appreciation, washing the whole thing down with half a pot of sweetened coffee.

Cassie, however, picked at her food. She smiled from time to time and held up her end of the conversation, but it was plain that she was deeply troubled.

Figuring that she would want to turn in early, Fargo drained his last cup shortly before eight o'clock, then sighed contentedly. "If nothing else," he said, "you could always get work as a cook. That was one of the finest meals I've eaten in a long time."

Memories made Cassie's face glimmer with happiness. "Simon used to praise my cooking, too." The moment passed, and she shrugged. "Who knows? Maybe I'll give it a try. There are worse jobs."

Fargo knew she was thinking of Prine. Patting his full stomach, he said, "You must want to turn in. I'd best be going."

Cassie started. "What? Why? I took it for granted that you would spend the night." She indicated the couch. "It's plenty big enough. Or you can use the bed again, if you want."

"I don't want to put you out on my account. There's a hayloft down at the stable I can use," Fargo revealed.

"Nonsense. I won't hear of it." Cassie's voice held a peculiar note that Fargo could not quite identify. "It's the least I can do after all you've done for us. So let's not hear any more about your leaving. Morning will be soon enough."

To avoid hurting her feelings any more than he already

had, Fargo agreed to stay. It was only one more night, and it would give him the chance to do something else for her he had in mind before he left.

They played cards until ten. Cassie kindled the fire. It was cozy sitting there warm and well fed with her and the baby. It reminded him why most men enjoyed married life so much, and why it was not for him.

The truth was, a week of wedded bliss would have Fargo climbing the walls with boredom. He had never been one to stay in any single place too long. Wanderlust was to blame, the constant urge to travel that had taken him from one end of the country to another and was always driving him to see what lay over the next horizon. He could no more change his ways than he could stop breathing.

But that did not mean Fargo looked down his nose on those who were different. No two men or women were alike. Each had to do what was best for them.

Cassie turned in, taking the crib into the bedroom with her. She brought Fargo several blankets and arranged them on the couch. "There. That should do you. If there is anything else you need, just give a holler." Acting nervous, she blew out the lantern. "Good night."

Fargo stripped off his boots and gun belt but left his clothes on. He intended to be up and gone before she was, or it would spoil the surprise he had in store. Making himself comfortable, he closed his eyes and listened to wood crackle in the fireplace. The meal had made him so drowsy that he had no trouble falling asleep.

Twice Fargo awoke. Once he thought that he heard scratching at the front door, but it was not repeated so he chalked it up as his imagination. The second time he came awake abruptly, certain that he was no longer alone in the room. A rustling sound confirmed it. Without being obvious, he lowered his right arm toward the floor, where his gun belt lay.

A finger brushed his lips.

"Please. Don't say anything."

Fargo looked up. Cassie was bent over him, her face wreathed by shadow, a gray blanket draped over her slender shoulders. A fragrance he had not noticed before tingled his nostrils. She quickly, nervously, pecked him on the lips. "There's no need—" he tried to say, but she covered his mouth with her entire palm.

"Don't say anything," she repeated. "Not one word. I want to, and that's all that counts. Tomorrow we'll go our separate ways with no regrets."

"Are you sure?" Fargo could not resist asking when she slid onto the couch on top of him, straddling his waist.

"Are any of us ever sure of anything?" Cassie whispered. "I've been lying in there for hours debating what to do. My heart says one thing and my head says another." She leaned down and kissed the tip of his jaw. "Simon would never forgive me, but Simon is gone now and I have to live for myself. Maybe the sooner I realize that, the better off I'll be." She nibbled at his throat, then licked him.

Fargo had never turned down a lovely woman before, but he did not want to have her conscience plague her with guilt forever after. He gave her one last chance to back out. "I didn't come here expecting this. I bought the groceries because you needed them."

"I know," Cassie whispered tenderly. "If you'd had an ulterior motive, I wouldn't be sitting here." She molded her chest to his. "Now, be quiet and kiss me, silly, before the baby wakes up and I have to go."

Fargo did as she wanted. Her lips were incredibly soft, incredibly pliant. They parted, and her silken tongue darted into his mouth to dance a slow, passionate waltz with his. As the kiss lingered, a throaty purr fluttered from Cassie, a purr that gradually became a hungry growl. Her hands roved over his shoulders, up his neck, and into his hair.

Fargo started to slide the blanket off her shoulders. Bare skin glistened in the flickering glow of firelight. She was naked! Her shoulders were exposed, then her arms, and finally her pendulous breasts, which swayed enticingly as she shifted her mouth to his ear and bit on the lobe.

Creamy flesh yielded to Fargo's ardent touch as he ran a hand from her marble throat to her right nipple. It was swollen with lust, as hard as the head of a nail, and she shivered when he lightly pinched it between his forefinger and thumb. His other hand found her other breast and gave it the same treatment.

Cassie's growl grew in volume. She was starved for affection, and she could not get enough of him. Her hands were everywhere, rubbing and stroking and massaging. Her hot mouth favored his with repeated kisses.

Fargo heard her gasp when he cupped both mounds and squeezed. She was remarkedly sensitive there, more so than most women. As he kneaded her, her breathing grew heavier and heavier until she panted as if she had just run a footrace. Her hips mashed against his, her legs rubbed his ribs. His groin twitched, his manhood hardening. Soon it was safe to say that he desired her as much as she craved him.

"Oh, Skye," Cassie whispered when his hand drifted to her flat stomach. "I'm bubbling inside."

Fargo could tell. Her body gave off more heat than the stove had. His right hand dipped to the curly thatch of hair at the junction of her thighs, and she thrust her nether mound against him, rubbing herself as if she had an itch. He accommodated her by extending a finger into the folds of her nether lips, which elicited a prolonged sigh of supreme joy.

"Please, Skye. Please."

Not quite sure what she meant, Fargo slowly inserted his middle finger into her core. She was a cauldron, hot and wet and boiling with suppressed cravings. Her inner walls clung to him as he stroked her, gently at first, but with rising intensity.

"Oh, God!" Cassie husked. "I've missed it so!"

Fargo shifted, throwing the blanket that had covered her

to the floor, exposing her velvety legs and the contours of her alabaster thighs. She was exquisite, yet she did not realize it. His lips greedily swooped to her left breast, lathering the nipple.

The combination of his mouth and his finger had her wriggling and squirming in rampant delight. Cassie tilted so he could penetrate her even farther, her body rocking back and forth in time to the cadence of his thrusts. Her mouth glued to his, her hot breath caressed his cheek.

Presently, Cassie lifted herself to throw off his own blankets. She tore at his shirt, getting it off with difficulty, then applied herself to his pants, undoing his belt and hitching them down past his hips. It was the best she could do without getting off him, and it sufficed.

Fargo was surprised when her hands closed on his swollen member. Some women would touch a man there, others would not. He had pegged her as the reserved sort, but evidently he was wrong. She had no qualms about rubbing his pole from top to bottom and cradling his jewels.

"You're so huge!" she exclaimed.

Little did she know he was not yet fully aroused. Fargo added a second finger to the first, doubling her pleasure. Head thrown back, mouth agape in carnal abandon, she braced her left foot on the floor to give her better leverage when she pumped against him.

Fargo's pole grew to its full length. Her body slapping against his stomach, Cassie encircled it with her left hand. She tossed her head from side to side, her cherry lips forming a delectable oval, her eyes hooded. He licked her other breast, bit her shoulder. Together they were climbing to the peak of passion, and it was only a matter of time before one of them exploded.

As much as Fargo wanted to, he held himself in check for her benefit. She was the one in need of release. Gripping her by the hips, he raised her off his chest until she was suspended above his erect organ. Then, carefully, he lowered her down again, impaling her to the hilt.

For a few moments Cassie merely sat there, her chest heaving. A short cry escaped her, the signal for her to churn against him as if trying to mash him into the couch. The satiny sensation brought him to the brink, stretching his self-control to its limits.

"Oh! Oh! Oh!" Cassie cooed. "I never—! I just never—!"

Fargo felt her walls contract, felt her womanhood grip his manhood in a prelude of the flood to come. Moments later she gushed like a geyser, her body as taut as a bowstring, her arms folded across her own chest, her features a study in rapture. She plunged and bucked so violently that he had to hold onto her or she would have fallen off.

Driving up into her again and again, Fargo reached his own summit. He was spent of energy when they finally coasted to a stop and she collapsed on top of him, her satisfied smile his reward for being patient.

"Thank you," Cass said softly. "You have no idea what that meant to me."

Maybe he did. Fargo hugged her and closed his eyes, drifting into a peaceful slumber. He could not say exactly how much time had elapsed when the wail of the infant brought him briefly around. Cassie was sliding off. She hurriedly collected her blanket, pressed her lips against his cheek, then padded off.

When next Fargo opened his eyes, dawn was imminent. Pulling on his clothes, he buckled his gun belt and slipped into his boots. The fire had burned down to a few meager flames, which he rekindled so the room would be warm when Cassie woke up. Peeking into the bedroom, he found her asleep on the bed with little Shawn bundled in her arms.

Fargo took the wad of bills from his pocket. He counted out a hundred, paused, and added another fifty. It was about half of the stage fare she needed. Before he was through in Minnesota, he would see what he could do about getting her the rest.

Pink and yellow streaks framed the eastern horizon as Fargo made his way to the stable. The owner was up and about, feeding the animals, and he swung the double doors wide as Fargo saddled the Ovaro. Shoving the Henry into the boot, Fargo stepped into the stirrups and rode on out, bearing northward, to where a winding ribbon of a road entered dense woodland. Here he halted to await his friend.

Fargo did not have long to wait before the snort of horses, the drum of hooves, and the rattle of accoutrements heralded the arrival of the Army patrol. Captain Beckworth was at the head of nineteen troopers riding two abreast. Behind them trotted twelve members of the Minnesota Militia.

Of special interest to Fargo was the man riding beside the captain. Major Mortimer Gatz wore a saber in a silver scabbard, and had a pistol on his left hip. Preoccupied, chatting with Beckworth, Gatz had no idea Fargo was there until the patrol slowed at the captain's command and he faced forward to learn why.

Fargo kneed the Ovaro into position alongside Beckworth. Ignoring Gatz, who looked as if he had just swallowed a handful of walnuts still in their shells, he said, "Morning, Jim. Any new word on the Santees who hit the wood detail?"

"Only that their trail led toward Leech Lake, which is where Red Wing is camped," Beckworth revealed. Turning to Gatz, he said, "Major, allow me to introduce—"

"I know who this man is," Gatz said stiffly, "and I demand to know why a civilian is coming along. This is strictly a military matter. Send him away."

Beckworth did not hide his surprise. "Mr. Fargo is here at the request of Colonel Williams. His expertise in Indian affairs will be of considerable help when we question the Sioux."

"Expertise?" Major Gatz said venomously. "Since when does living with a squaw qualify a man as an expert? If anything, it should make his motives suspect. Perhaps his sympathies lie with the red vermin, not where they should."

"That's a base accusation," Beckworth responded. "I've known him far longer than you have, and I'll vouch for his integrity any day of the week." The captain paused. "If my word isn't enough, keep in mind that the Army has relied on Mr. Fargo countless times in his capacity as a scout and in other regards. He has never let us down."

"How wonderful," Gatz said dryly. "But the fact remains that I outrank you, Captain, and I insist that this man not accompany us."

Fargo was going to speak in his own defense, but Jim Beckworth beat him to it.

"Who do you think you are? First off, Major, you appointed yourself to that rank. As a duly commissioned federal officer, I have the authority here. Secondly, I thought Colonel Williams made it clear that the only reason he let you come along was as a gesture of goodwill." Beckworth had his dander up, and he jabbed Gatz in the arm. "So don't let me hear you give an order again, mister. As for Fargo, he stays whether you like it or not."

On that friendly note, the patrol got underway. Major Gatz promptly joined his militiamen, and they kept to themselves the remainder of the day. That evening, Gatz had his men set up a separate camp near the Army camp rather than combine the two forces.

"That man is the biggest jackass who ever lived," Captain Beckworth remarked as Fargo and he sat sipping coffee under twinkling stars. "Why didn't you tell me that you knew him?"

"It didn't seem important at the time," Fargo fibbed.

"Why does he hate you so much?"

"Ask him," Fargo hedged. If his friend were to learn the truth, Beckworth was liable to send the militiamen packing. And Fargo had plans for Major Mortimer Gatz.

"Suit yourself, but this assignment is too crucial for me to tolerate any bickering between the two of you. If there's any trouble, any at all, my men and I will go on alone."

It was a four-day ride to Fort Ripley if they pushed, and push Beckworth did. As he confided on the second morning, he was under strict orders to deal with the crisis promptly.

"Washington is worried sick that the Santees will get their hands on more repeaters before we can plug the source. That could lead to full-scale war," he reported. "They can't spare more troops for the frontier when some of the Southern states might secede from the Union any day now."

Fargo rode ahead of the column most of the time, alert for sign. The only evidence of Indians were old unshod tracks that crossed the road at one point. But he did find something that sparked his curiosity.

A wagon had left Minneapolis a day ahead of them. The width of the wheels and their depth hinted at a freight wagon bearing its load limit. Fargo mentioned the discovery to Beckworth that evening as they ate supper.

"Odd," the officer said. "Fort Snelling is the relay point for supplies to Fort Ripley and our other remote posts. So I know for a fact that the regular supply run isn't for another two weeks. Who else would be hauling up this way?" Snapping his fingers, he leaped to his feet, so excited that he spilled some of his stew. "It must be the gun traffickers!"

The same thought had occurred to Fargo. "Maybe," he said. "Or it could be someone who works for a logging outfit."

Beckworth dismissed the notion with a wave. "The loggers don't cut this far north for fear of the Sioux." He paced in a small circle. "Whoever it is, they can't be very far ahead of us. I'd like for you to overtake the wagon tomorrow, Skye, then report back on what you find."

Fargo turned in early to be refreshed for the hard ride. He was gone before most of the troopers were awake. Mortimer Gatz was one of those up, and the bigot glared openly while fingering the hilt of his saber.

Four miles farther Fargo found where the freighter had stopped for the night. The campfire was still warm. Encouraged, he proceeded at a gallop for two more miles, at which point he crested a rise and saw his quarry barreling along a straight section of road below. Hundreds of yards separated them, but there was no mistaking the driver.

Whipping in the brisk wind was a mane of lustrous red hair.

6

Skye Fargo wished it had been someone other than Wagon Annie. He recalled how strangely she had behaved after learning he was there to help the Army find those responsible for arming the Santees, and now he wondered if there was a link.

The possible motive was plain. Her small freight line was competing with Wallace Freighting for business. With her drivers gone, she was having a hard time staying afloat. Given how she had acted at Fort Snelling the other day, she must be in dire need of money.

There was a flaw, though, to Fargo's reasoning. The Sioux had none to offer her, or so everyone claimed. But what if they were wrong? he reflected. What if the Santees had somehow laid their hands on enough?

The answer was in that wagon. Fargo waited until it had gone around a bend before he followed. He would give Annie the benefit of the doubt, and shadow her for a while. There was no rush. She could not outrun him, and the patrol would not catch up with them for quite some time yet.

As usual, Annie held the team to a reckless pace. She took turns much too fast, and her whip seldom stopped cracking on the straight stretches. Two miles farther she did slow down, only because she had to negotiate a series of steep grades.

Fargo plunged into the trees and narrowed the gap between them to less than twenty yards. The risk of being spotted was much greater, but he wanted to get a good look at her load. The bed had been filled halfway, then covered by a canvas sheet that flapped at one end, affording him an occasional peek at stacked boxes and a lot of bulging burlap sacks.

In addition to the freight, the wagon carried a water keg and a tar bucket for greasing the running gear. On long treks some freighters would throw on an extra tongue, yoke, and axle in case of a mishap, but Annie had not seen fit to bring any along.

The noon hour came and went. Wagon Annie did not stop to rest her mules, which soon showed signs of flagging. Fargo was surprised she could be so heartless. Most bull whackers put the welfare of their animals above all else. And since it would take her another day and a half to reach the fort, she needed to keep her team in top condition.

The road grew steadily worse, narrowing until it was barely wide enough for the wagon to get by. Deep ruts had been worn in the soil, causing the bed to constantly lurch and sway.

It was close to two in the afternoon when Wagon Annie unexpectedly halted. She glanced both ways to insure no one was in sight, then hopped down and stepped to the right side of the road. For a few seconds she studied the wall of vegetation, as if seeking something.

Fargo assumed she was going off into the bushes to heed Nature's call. So he was all the more confounded when she reached into what appeared to be a dense, tangled thicket, and seemed to slide a section of the "thicket" to the right. It was actually a crude latticework cleverly layered with small limbs and leaves so that it blended into the vegetation.

Even more fascinating was the reason the latticework had been constructed. As wide as the wagon and about six feet high, it concealed a rutted track that veered off into the forest. Annie wasted no time bounding onto the wagon and guiding her team off the main road. Stopping again, she closed the opening, arranging the cover so artfully that no one giving it a casual glance would ever guess it existed.

Fargo listened as the creaks and clatterings of the wagon receded in the distance. When Annie was safely gone, he crossed the road and paralleled the rutted track she had taken. Grass had filled in some of the ruts, which told him that the offshoot was infrequently used.

Wagon Annie was going much slower. She had no choice. The track twisted and turned, trees growing so close that often they scraped her wagon. It wound into a narrow, wooded valley bordered by low hills. Around another bend she came on a wide clearing flanked by a gurgling creek. Here she wheeled the team into a semicircle, turning them so they were pointed at the rutted track.

Screened by white pines, Fargo watched her climb down and stretch to relieve a kink in her back. She busied herself unhitching the mules, and tethered them near the water so they could drink when they wanted. Her next order of business was a small fire. He took note when she reached under the seat and produced a coiled gun belt and holster. It was the first time he had seen her with a gun. She strapped it on and drew the pistol to check the cylinder.

A Smith & Wesson .44-caliber, Fargo observed. A big, heavy revolver, but he had no doubt she was as capable with it as she was with her bullwhip. The lady did nothing halfway.

Annie scanned the trees, not once but three times, as if she sensed that she was being watched. Shoving the Smith & Wesson back in its holster, she walked to the bed, slid a hand under the canvas, and pulled out a rifle, a seven-shot Spencer. It must have been already loaded, because she did not bother to do so.

Now well armed, Annie took a beaded buffalo-hide bag from the bed and sat by the fire. The bag was of special interest to Fargo. It was called a parfleche. Indians used them all the time to store things. No two tribes fashioned theirs exactly the same, and the style of Annie's parfleche revealed that it had been constructed by the Sioux.

Where had she gotten it? Fargo wondered, afraid that the

evidence against her was mounting by the moment. Since it looked as if she had settled in for a long wait, he did the same. Dismounting, he stripped off his saddle. Taking a handful of jerky from his saddlebags, he sat with his back propped against a trunk and resumed spying on the possible turncoat.

Annie was fixing herself coffee. She munched on a small cake while she waited for the pot to come to a boil. Once, in the undergrowth on the other side of the creek, a twig snapped. She leaped up, leveling the Spencer, her relief obvious when a doe stepped into the open. She ran off on seeing the wagon.

Fargo chewed thoughtfully. She was as nervous as a prairie dog in a rattlesnake den. Either she was just being naturally cautious, or whoever she was waiting for posed a threat.

The afternoon waned. Captain Beckworth would worry if Fargo failed to show up by sunset, but Fargo was not going anywhere until he learned what Annie was up to. If more Henrys were in that wagon, he would stop her from passing them on to the Santees.

The Henry was a remarkable rifle. Manufactured by the New Haven Repeating Arms Company, it was a rimfire .44-caliber masterpiece. Fifteen shots were held in a tubular magazine under the barrel. All a man had to do to extract a spent cartridge and insert a new one was work a lever that also served as a trigger guard. In the hands of someone who knew how to use one, it could fire thirty shots a minute, a tremendous improvement on the old single-shot Sharps and twice the rate of fire of a Spencer.

Many frontiersmen had done as Fargo did and traded in their Sharps for the new Henrys when the new rifles first came out. What man could afford not to, since, as an old-timer had joked, "you can load the Henry on Sunday and shoot it all week." An added incentive was the Henry's stopping power. While it did not have the wallop of a .50-caliber Sharps, it could penetrate a five-inch board at four hundred yards. That was more than enough to bring down any man or animal that lived.

A disaster would result if the Santees got their hands on a lot of them. Fifty Henrys were equal to seven hundred and fifty single-shot rifles. And that was exactly what the troopers on the frontier were armed with. For the Army ordnance board, in its infinite wisdom, had not yet ruled the Henry or even the Spencer adequate for military use. Soldiers had to rely on single-shot Sharps rifles and carbines, where they were available. In many instances, lack of funds meant that the troops carried cheaply made percussion rifles and muskets.

Fifty Santees armed with Henrys could drive the Army from Minnesota.

Fargo finished his jerky. The sun was poised on the rim of the world, the shadows lengthening by the second. Soon it was gone, and twilight spread across the wilderness. Wagon Annie broke out a can of beans and some bread.

Just when Fargo figured that whoever she was waiting for would not show up until the next day, the crunch and thud of heavy hooves in timber to the northwest brought Annie to her feet again, with the Spencer wedged to her shoulder. He rose also, palming the Colt. Riders materialized, vague shapes at first. Dreading who they would be, Fargo crept closer.

Out of high weeds rode a tall warrior on a warhorse. The way he wore his long raven hair, his leggings and moccasins, his bow and quiver, and his bone-handled knife, pegged him as a Santee Sioux. Four more emerged, and stayed on their mounts while their leader swung lithely down and approached the redhead.

Wagon Annie had not lowered the Spencer. "I brought the stuff on time, just like I promised," she declared.

The warrior stopped. Pointing at her rifle, he said in thickly accented English, "There is no need for that."

"Isn't there?" Annie countered. "I heard about your boys and that wood detail. How do I know I can trust you?"

Folding his arms, the warrior said, "After all you have done for my people, Red Hair, why would I turn on you? We are friends, are we not?"

"I thought so, but now I ain't so sure," Annie responded. "It won't be long before your people are taking scalps right and left. I don't want one of them to be mine."

The warrior debated a moment, then made a show of depositing each of his weapons on the ground. "To prove that I mean you no harm. Now can we sit and smoke the pipe of friendship?"

Annie glanced at the quartet behind him. "What about them? The only one I recognize is Long Fish. What's to keep one of the others from putting an arrow into my back the minute it's turned?"

"You wound my heart, my sister," the warrior said earnestly. "My people all know what you have done for us. None would ever raise a finger against you."

"So you claim," Annie said, but she let the barrel of the Spencer droop. "All right. Plant yourself. But have those others keep their distance. I'm awful sorry, but I don't know who to trust anymore."

The stately warrior did as she requested. From a bag slung over his shoulder, he took a beautifully carved pipe and began to fill the bowl with tobacco. His gaze drifted to the wagon. "You brought everything?"

"Don't I always?" Annie retorted. She had squatted with the rifle across her hips. "You have no idea what I had to go through this time to keep it a secret. It gets harder every trip. And it will only get worse if your people go on the warpath."

Fargo frowned, keenly disappointed. What more proof did he need? Her own words convicted her. It was too bad. He liked her, liked her a lot. Flattening, he circled to the left, crawling at a turtle's pace.

The four warriors across the clearing had dismounted and taken seats on the grass. Two were armed with bows, one with a lance, another with a fusee, a single-shot trade gun with a cracked stock that had been repaired by wrapping a piece of leather around it. None showed much interest in the talk their leader was having.

The tall warrior was tamping the tobacco. "My heart will be sad when that day comes," he was saying. "It was long my hope that our two peoples could live in peace. But now I see that this can never be. Your kind hate mine. They want to drive us from the land hunted by our fathers and our fathers' fathers."

"Not all of us do," Annie said.

"Most," the warrior stated flatly. "Just as most of mine will no longer accept being treated as if we are dogs. Whites beat us, lie to us, cheat us. They want us to do as the Winnebagos have done and live on a reservation, as you call it. But we are not Winnebagos, to be penned like cattle."

Fargo was aware that over a decade ago the Santees had signed a treaty they had not fully understood, ceding twenty-four million acres of their former territory to the U.S. government. Many of them had honored the treaty and moved onto a small reservation. But of late more and more were breaking away and going off to live in the wilds.

The tall warrior was growing agitated, his voice rising. "Do you know, Red Hair, that Myrick, the store owner, has refused to give my people any more credit? He told my wife that when game is scarce and our little ones are hungry, they should eat grass!"

"You still have friends among my kind," Wagon Annie said. "Bishop Whipple has written to Washington many times begging them to honor the treaty."

"And has the Great White Father listened to White Collar?" The Santee gestured sharply. "He has not! So my people gnash their teeth in misery, and long for the day when the whites will leave our country forever."

"Be patient," Wagon Annie said. "Bishop Whipple will get results eventually."

"We weary of waiting," the warrior said, and looked at

the wagon. "The time is near for us to act. I would like to see what you have brought."

Shrugging, Annie moved to the freight wagon and threw back the canvas. "Take a gander. There's not as much as I would have liked. It should be enough, though, to last for several months; even if you use it up fast."

The tall warrior set down the pipe and stood. "By then blood will be spilled."

It sounded to Fargo as if they were discussing ammunition. He was within a yard or so of the clearing and about halfway between the fire and the four warriors.

"We have packhorses in the trees," the Santee leader disclosed. "We will load them in the morning and go our own way."

"The sooner, the better," Annie said. "I need to get back to Minneapolis before anyone gets suspicious. If my people should learn what I've been up to, my life won't be worth a flake of fool's gold."

The pair peered into the wagon while the quartet looked on. Fargo picked that moment to spring into the open, brandishing the Colt. "I'd like a look in there myself," he declared.

Wagon Annie and her tall friend whirled. Annie's hand dropped to her Smith & Wesson. The four Sioux leaped to their feet, one elevating a lance to hurl it. A word from the leader stopped him, and for several moments the tableau was frozen.

"I don't believe it!" Annie broke the strained silence. "What the hell are you doing here, Skye?"

Fargo warily advanced, swinging the Colt toward the four warriors and back again. "I should be asking you the same question," he said, "but then, I think I know the answer." Shifting sideways so he could keep one eye on the Sioux, he directed, "Stand back. And take your hand off that .44."

Annie hesitated. "This is personal business. It doesn't concern you, damn it!"

"So you say," Fargo countered. The tall Sioux was studying him closely, but had not made any hostile moves. "I'd be more inclined to believe you if you hadn't gone to so much trouble to set up this secret meeting place with the Santees." He nodded at the wagon. "What's in there, Annie? It wouldn't be Henry rifles by any chance?"

"Is that what you think?" Wagon Annie rejoined, and took a step toward him with her fists clenched. "Why, you mangy polecat! I should box your ears in for that insult."

Fargo reached the side and peeked in. One of the burlap sacks had opened, revealing containers of salt. He untwisted the top of another. It held flour. A third had been crammed with sugar, a fourth with beans. "All food," he declared.

"Naturally," Annie said smugly. "Now, open one of the boxes, why don't you, and tell me what you find."

None of the Santees had moved. Fargo held the Colt steady on their leader as he climbed into the bed. The first crate was filed with canned goods. The second had folded blankets in it. Another was near bursting with woolen shirts and pants.

Wagon Annie was smirking. "Satisfied, busybody? I'd no more sell guns to the Indians than I would sell my soul to the devil."

"Someone has been," Fargo remarked, unwilling to accept that she had gone to so much trouble merely to sell goods to the Sioux. "Why didn't you have them meet you closer to town if this is all you were up to?"

"Brilliant idea," Wagon Annie said. "Why didn't I think of that?" She laughed at his expense. "Could it be that there are so many loggers and settlers flocking into the countryside around Minneapolis, someone was bound to spot us? Could that be why we picked this out-of-the-way place?"

Fargo rummaged through several more boxes and bags, with the same result. "It's all food and clothing," he marveled. "They could get this anywhere."

"Do you have turnips growing between your ears?"

Annie said. "If you were eavesdropping, then you heard about Myrick, the storekeeper. No one will sell the Sioux anything. Yet our government demands that they give up hunting and live just like we do."

Fargo holstered the Colt and leaned on the side. The discovery gladdened him more than he would admit. Ann Standley wasn't the gun trafficker, after all. "So you've been making a little money on the side by selling merchandise to the Santees that they can't get anywhere else."

The tall leader spoke. "Red Hair does not ask for money. She gives from the goodness of her heart."

"What?" Fargo said, genuinely surprised. Here was a whole new side to Wagon Annie, a side no one else knew existed.

"It's nothing much," the redhead declared, her cheeks darkening to match the color of her hair.

"Three times each year she does this, white man," the Santee said. "Her food has fed us in the winter when we were starving. Her clothes warm our children when the cold wind blows."

Fargo was mystified. "Why keep it a secret?" he asked the firebrand. "Most folks like to crow about their good deeds."

Wagon Annie grew pensive. "You know how most of the people in these parts feel about Indians. Anyone who treats them decent is branded as an Indian lover and treated as if they have the plague." She patted the freight wagon. "I can't afford that. If I lose too many clients, I'm out of business."

"I see your point," Fargo said. If her rival, Ed Wallace, ever found out, he would use the information to ruin her. "Well, don't fret there. My lips are sealed."

"Enough about me," Wagon Annie said. She motioned at the warrior. "Skye Fargo, make the acquaintance of Red Wing, one of the top Santee chiefs. Only Little Crow and Medicine Bottle have more influence among his people than he does."

"Come," the warrior said, beckoning. "Smoke with us. I will tell you more about Red Hair, and how she came to help us as she does."

"There's no need—" Wagon Annie started to respond, her objection drowned out by the sudden crashing of horses in the underbrush as a half-dozen additional Santee warriors burst into the clearing, then spread out. The four over by the creek leaped to their feet and raced to the wagon to plant themselves in front of Red Wing.

Fargo stayed where he was, his right hand close to his pistol. Judging by the chief's reaction, this was not a welcome development.

The newcomers were led by a young warrior whose swarthy features were marred by a jagged scar that creased his left eyelid and part of his left cheek. Clutched in his right hand was a shiny new Henry. The warriors with him also held new repeaters. Scowling, the young Santee raked the five Sioux by the wagon with a scornful look, then fixed on Red Wing.

"So this is where you go when you disappear from our village? I should have known. You take handouts from this white cur, and our people think you have powerful medicine."

Red Wing shouldered past the warriors who were protecting him. "You followed us against my wishes, Fire Thunder."

The name jarred Fargo's memory. Fire Thunder was the name of the warrior responsible for inciting the Sioux to wage war, the warrior who had led the band that attacked the wood detail out of Fort Ripley, the man Captain Beckworth had been sent to apprehend. Automatically, Fargo started to reach for his pistol. The sight of three Henrys trained on his chest changed his mind. Annie, he saw, was covered by two others.

"A Santee can do as he pleases," Fire Thunder said arrogantly. "We are not so like the whites yet that we bow and kiss the feet of those who would be our leaders."

Red Wing scanned the men who rode with the renegade. "What of you, Runs Against? And you, Makes Room? Or you, Killing Ghost? You have always heeded my counsel in the past. Why oppose me now?"

A stocky warrior answered. "You say that war will come, but tell us to be patient. It is not the right time, you say. But when will the right time be? When our people have no land left? When most of us are dead?"

"The Great Mystery will give us a sign," Red Wing said. "Until then, we do the best we can to survive."

Fire Thunder snorted like a bull buffalo. "Talk, talk, talk. That is all the older ones are good for. And look what it has brought us! The whites overrun our land. They kill our game." He shook his Henry in the air. "I say enough, my brothers! I say we must reclaim what is ours! The time to kill whites is now! Let us make an example of these two."

With that, Fire Thunder took a slow, deliberate bead on Wagon Annie.

7

Skye Fargo did not stand a prayer against six repeating rifles, but he could not stand there and do nothing while Wagon Annie was shot down in cold blood. He tensed to throw himself from the wagon and knock her aside, but before he could leap, someone else intervened.

Squaring his shoulders, Red Wing stepped in front of the redhead. "This woman is my friend," he declared. "To kill her, Fire Thunder, you must first kill me."

The renegade jerked his head up. "Move aside. You do not have the right to stop me."

Red Wing held his ground. To the other warriors he said, "Red Hair's kindness has spared our people much suffering and saved many lives. Is this how we show our gratitude? If it is, we are no better than those whites who would slay us for no other reason than the color of our skin is different."

One of the men who had arrived with Fire Thunder lowered his weapon. "Red Wing speaks truth. The whites who hate us are our enemies, not those who treat us kindly."

Fire Thunder glared at the speaker. "You, too, Killing Ghost? I thought you were a warrior, not an old woman."

Another Santee lowered his rifle. "I, Runs Against, have more reason than most to want the whites dead. They killed my brother and my uncle. But it is wrong to cut off a hand offered in friendship. This woman's food kept my children alive last winter. I will not harm her."

"Waugh!" Fire Thunder growled. "I am surrounded by old women!" Furious, he swung his Henry toward Fargo.

"What of this white man, then? He has not given our people anything. Let us take him and test his courage."

Fargo pivoted so he was facing the renegade. He would rather be filled with lead than submit to torture, and he would make it a point to take Fire Thunder with him. Three of the warriors kneed their warhorses closer, coming at him from different angles. They were ready to shoot if he went for his gun, which he was on the verge of doing, when through the trees galloped two more Santees, young warriors who made straight for Fire Thunder.

"We went to see about the campfires in the distance," one reported, "and found many bluecoats."

"That is not all," said the other. "With them are twelve browncoats. One is the man you hate so much, the white who beat Lame Deer with a stick."

Fire Thunder looked at his Henry, and Fargo could guess what the hotheaded Santee was thinking. Gunshots carried far on the night wind. The soldiers were bound to hear and investigate. "We go," he curtly announced, then stared at Fargo. "This one can wait. We will find him again easily enough."

Just like that the war party was gone, filing silently into the woods except for the dull drum of hooves, which rapidly faded. Wagon Annie pushed her hat back and arched an eyebrow at Fargo. "We were lucky, you know that? For a minute there, I figured we were both goners."

Red Wing put a hand on her shoulder. "You need have no fear so long as you are with me. I will not let anyone harm you, Red Hair."

Fargo sprang to the ground. He was torn between staying to look after Annie or going to warn Beckworth that the renegades were in the area. "I have to leave," he said.

"Are you loco?" the redhead said. "With Fire Thunder and his bunch roaming around out there? What if you run into them?"

Already around the wagon and halfway to the pines, Fargo glanced over a shoulder. "Then, there will be hell to pay. But you can count on me being back in the morning to give you a hand."

Annie's features softened. "I'd like that, handsome," she said. "Maybe it was wrong of me not to confide in you from the start; but trusting folks doesn't come easy for me."

"That makes two of us." Fargo jogged into the woods, and weaved through the boles and brush until he spotted the stallion. Quickly throwing on the saddle blanket and saddle, he lit out at a trot. Although few tribes waged war at night, he wouldn't put it past Fire Thunder to pick off a few soldiers just for the hell of it.

The rutted track enabled Fargo to go faster. He slowed when he judged that he was in the vicinity of the latticework that hid the track. Soon a shadowy mass loomed before him, and he slanted into the vegetation to go around it.

Since the patrol had to be somewhere north of him, Fargo swung to the left on reaching the main road and brought the Ovaro to a gallop. He had gone only a mile or so when flickering pinpoints of light flared in the distance. Twists and turns hid them most of the time, but soon he could distinguish the flames of two campfires and vague shapes passing back and forth in front of them.

It appeared that Beckworth had pitched camp in a meadow bordering the road to the east. Fire Thunder's band was bound to be lurking nearby, so again Fargo slowed, holding the stallion to a walk to avoid drawing unwanted attention.

The final hundred yards would be the riskiest. That was when the Sioux would try to stop him if they had warriors posted south of the encampment. Fargo reined up, slid off, and palmed the Colt. Leading the pinto by the reins, he glided along the edge of the road, doubled over to present a smaller target.

Something rustled in the trees. Fargo paused, probing every shadow. Spying no cause for alarm, he crept on.

Beckworth was bound to have sentries posted, and he would be challenged at any moment. He straightened to better see the road ahead, and too late heard the pad of moccasin-shod feet almost at his right elbow.

A battering ram slammed into Fargo's side. A knife sheared at his face, but by a sheer fluke he blocked it as he fell, the blade ringing off the barrel of his revolver, which went flying. Fargo landed on his side and rolled into a crouch. In front of him, also crouched to spring, was one of the warriors who had been with Fire Thunder.

The young Santee closed. Fargo hurled himself backward, evading a slash that would have opened his neck from ear to ear. His right hand slipped into his right boot, his fingers molding around the hilt of the Arkansas toothpick. It streaked clear in time to parry another thrust.

The young Sioux danced to one side, more cautious but just as determined to end Fargo's life. They circled, each dancing out of the way of flicking steel.

Fargo had to end the fight quickly. Other warriors might be nearby and come to his foe's aid. He saw that a tree was behind the Santee, and lunged. The warrior did as Fargo intended and backpedaled, colliding with the trunk. As the man pivoted to get in the clear, Fargo was on him, driving the toothpick low even as he delivered an uppercut with his left fist.

The gambit worked. The warrior was so intent on blocking the toothpick that he never saw the fist coming. It rammed into his jaw, jolting him, causing him to go momentarily weak in the knees. It was all the opening Fargo needed. A foot to the groin doubled the warrior over. Hard knuckles slammed into the base of the Santee's skull, ending their clash.

Fargo rotated, seeking more enemies. When none materialized, he searched for the Colt. Once he had it in hand, he replaced the toothpick and bent to the task of hoisting the warrior onto his shoulder. Then he draped the body over his saddle. Somewhere to the left an owl hooted and was answered by another farther away. If they were real owls, he was the Queen of England.

Reclaiming the reins, he hurried toward the nearest fire. He assumed it was Beckworth's until he was gruffly hailed, and a figure dressed in brown popped out of the darkness, nervously wagging a rifle.

"Halt and identify yourself, mister!"

Fargo had wanted to slip into the Army camp quietly. Now every Santee within earshot knew he had arrived, and soon they would recognize his burden. "Quiet down, boy," he snapped. "And quit pointing that gun at me. It's liable to go off."

The sentry backed up a step, but did not lower the rifle. "I told you to identify yourself!" he demanded.

"You know damn well who I am," Fargo responded. The militiaman was no more than seventeen or eighteen, as green as grass and as brazen as a bull. "I've been with the patrol since it left Minneapolis,"

"I have to follow procedure," the sentry said stiffly, then bawled out, "Major Gatz, sir! Sentry post three! On the double, please!"

In no mood to be trifled with, Fargo started to walk on past the martinet and had the rifle muzzle shoved in front of his nose.

The boy's skin glistened with sweat, and he licked his thin lips. "I'm warning you, mister! I have my orders."

Militiamen converged on the run, foremost among them Major Mortimer Gatz. The living brick wall planted himself in front of Fargo, and rested a hand on the hilt of his saber. "Well, well, well. What have we here? Where have you been all day?"

"None of your damn business," Fargo said. He owed them no explanation, and after what they had done to him the other night, he was not going to let them run roughshod over him. Brushing past Gatz, he headed toward the other campfire, but had his path barred by several husky militiamen. "Out of my way," he said.

"Stay where you are, men," Major Gatz said, inspecting the unconscious warrior as he moved around in front of

Fargo again. "Isn't this interesting. You've taken a prisoner. As the head of this detachment of the Minnesota Militia, I demand that you turn him over to me this instant."

"Like hell I will," Fargo said.

Gatz, sneering, motioned at the husky bruisers. "Privates, relieve this civilian of the savage. If he resists, we'll clap leg irons on him for obstructing a duly appointed field commander in the performance of his duties."

The three men fanned out. Fargo couldn't be sure, but he suspected they were the same ones who had been with Gatz when he was jumped near Cassie's cabin. The one in the middle cocked his rifle to swing the stock, but the blow never landed.

A wedge of federal troopers plowed into the militiamen, scattering them like corn husks in a high wind. Captain Beckworth stomped up to Major Gatz and thrust a finger into the major's gut. "What is the meaning of this outrage? Our scout comes back, and you threaten to manhandle him? Are you insane, or just stupid?"

Gatz reacted in typical fashion. "Your conduct, not mine, sir, is unbecoming for an officer. I have the authority to deal with any savages we find as I see fit, and I want this one for questioning."

"This is the last straw," Beckworth said. "Colonel Williams can court-martial me if he wants, but I refuse to tolerate your asinine behavior any longer. Effective at first light, we will go our separate ways. My patrol will proceed on to Fort Ripley, while you, Major, will return to Minneapolis."

Mortimer Gatz sputtered like a keg of powder about to explode. "No lowly captain can tell me what to do! I refuse to submit to your authority! We will go where I please, and if you don't like it, you are welcome to lodge a formal complaint with the governor."

Fargo felt sorry for his friend. It wasn't bad enough that Beckworth had to prevent a bloodbath that would paint the frontier red with blood, he also had to deal with fanatics like Gatz, who *craved* war. It didn't help any that the state and federal jurisdictions in the matter were blurred.

"Oh, the governor will hear about this, all right," Beckworth was saying. "So will the War Department. I intend to request that they exert what influence they can to have you stripped of your rank. You're as much a menace, sir, as the Santees."

Doing an about-face, Beckworth had his men form a protective ring around Fargo and the pinto. The militiamen looked to their leader, but Gatz made no attempt to stop the federal soldiers from leaving. Beckworth uttered a string of profanity, the likes of which Fargo had not heard in ages, concluding with, "It's next to hopeless, I tell you. How can they expect me to accomplish anything? Even if we catch the Sioux we're after, incompetents like Gatz will keep stirring things up until all hell breaks loose."

Fargo had to agree. The hatred on both sides was too intense. The Santees had suffered too many wrongs, and the whites were too greedy for the two sides to ever sit down and negotiate. The best Beckworth could hope to do was delay the inevitable a while longer. Exactly how long was anybody's guess.

"I have news about those Sioux you want," Fargo said quietly enough that the troopers ringing him could not overhear. "Fire Thunder and seven other warriors are watching us at this very moment."

To his credit, Captain Beckworth did not panic. Casually surveying the meadow and the forest, he said softly, "You wouldn't happen to know if the reports of them having Henrys are true?"

Fargo nodded. "Saw six repeaters with my own eyes. If they open fire, they'll cut down half of your detail before your men get off a shot."

Beckworth forced a grin. "Don't you ever get tired of always looking at the bright side?"

The commotion had brought every last soldier to his feet. They were clustered in a knot, blissfully ignorant of the tempting shots they presented to the concealed Sioux. Beckworth knew, though, and he snapped them to attention, posted additional sentries, and ordered that the fire be extinguished until further notice. The rest of the men were ordered to be prepared to fall in at a moment's notice.

Fargo's prisoner was bound and placed under guard. Fargo helped himself to what little coffee was left in the pot while it was still warm. Hunkering, he sipped, and listened to Gatz bellowing across the meadow. The militiamen were posting more sentries, too. They were also adding fuel to their fire instead of putting it out. He could see every one of them as plain as day.

Captain Beckworth came over. "I send you out after a freight wagon, and you come back with a renegade. Any connection?"

"No," Fargo hedged. "I caught up with the freighter, but the wagon wasn't carrying repeaters."

"Who was the driver?"

"I'd rather not say."

The officer was about to tug on a gauntlet. Pausing, he regarded Fargo soberly. "It's not like you to keep secrets, Skye. If the driver wasn't the gun trafficker, what harm can there be in revealing who it was?

If Beckworth only knew! Fargo reflected. The captain would accept his word that Annie was not the culprit. But what if word got back to Mortimer Gatz? The popinjay was not above hauling her in for questioning. Rumors would spread. The very thing that Annie feared, the loss of her business, would be the end result. "Let's just say that there are circumstances you don't know about, and let it go at that. When I can, I'll fill you in."

Beckworth was not pleased, but he did not press it. "I suppose that will have to do. In the meantime, what *can* you tell me?"

Briefly, Fargo related his encounter with Red Wing and Fire Thunder. "From what I've learned," he finished, "there are few renegades now, but their number will grow as time goes by."

"Colonel Williams thinks so, too. He's tried to make Washington come to its senses. But the stiff-necked bureaucrats there have pooh-poohed his suggestion that more troops be sent in to quell any potential uprising. They make light of the situation and accuse him of creating a mountain out of the proverbial molehill."

"They'll learn their lesson the hard way," Fargo predicted.

"Unfortunately, scores of innocents will pay with their lives before that happens." Sighing, Beckworth pulled on his other gauntlet. "Just between you and me, there are times when I'd like to take every politician in the country and fling them off a high cliff."

The officer went off to insure the perimeter was secure, leaving Fargo and two others to keep watch on the prisoner. By coincidence, the warrior abruptly revived. Sitting up, the Santee tore at the thick rope binding his bronzed wrists and ankles, but he could not budge them.

"Struggle all you want to," Fargo said in the Sioux tongue, "but you cannot free yourself."

The warrior refused to listen. Redoubling his efforts, he wore himself out striving to break loose. At length, nearly out of breath, his skin rubbed raw where the rope chafed his limbs, he slumped and asked, "What do your people plan to do with me, white man?"

"You will be taken to the wooden lodge of the bluecoats, north of here," Fargo revealed. "After that, it depends on the Army court of inquiry."

"Will they kill me?"

"That is not their way," Fargo said. "If you agree to live by the treaty, you could be sent back to your people. If not, they might lock you in a room for many moons. Or, if they find that you have killed any whites, they will send you far to the south, to a place called Florida, to what the white men call a prison. It has many iron bars on the windows and an iron gate to keep the prisoners from the outside world."

"I am a warrior!" the Sioux declared. "I will have my freedom, or I will give up my life."

Fargo felt little sympathy for the man. Being on the receiving end of a knife had that effect. Still, he could not help but think that the young warrior was more misguided than bloodthirsty. "You should not have let Fire Thunder sway your thoughts. He is the one who should be sent to prison."

"Why? Because he does what no other warrior would do? Because he stands up to your kind? Because he refuses to let them drive us from our land?" The warrior frowned. "There comes a time when a man, if he *is* a man, must rise against those who would destroy his way of life. Fire Thunder is but the first of many."

"He can't win. You must know that."

The Santee was quiet a few moments. "Is it the winning or the fight that is important? Maybe your kind will crush us as we crush bugs underfoot. But it will not be an easy victory. Your women will gnash their teeth and tear their dresses. Your men will talk of our prowess for many winters to come."

There was no making the warrior see reason, so Fargo did not try. The Sioux were too fired up to wage war. War, eventually, it would be, even if it cost them their limited freedom and lost them their reservation.

Captain Beckworth returned shortly with the news that "All's quiet at the moment. I have men posted at twenty-yard intervals. A mouse couldn't get in here without us knowing it."

Fargo had his doubts, but he did not express them. Since he had been on the go all day and needed some rest, he spread out his bedroll and reclined with the Henry at his side. The night proved uneventful, although whenever Fargo cracked his eyelids to scan the encampment, he swore that he could feel unfriendly eyes on him.

A golden sun crowned a glorious dawn. Fargo was adjusting the Ovaro's cinch when his friend appeared. "Leaving so soon? You haven't eaten any breakfast."

"I have something to do," Fargo said, and did not elaborate.

"It must be something in the air," Beckworth said. "All these early risers today."

"What do you mean?" Fargo asked, lowering the stirrup. "I should have been gone half an hour ago."

"You still would have lost out to Mortimer Gatz. Apparently, he and his boys slipped away in the middle of the night." Beckworth chuckled. "Frankly, I didn't think they had it in them."

Neither did Fargo. "Which way did they go?"

"I didn't check, but it had to be south," Captain Beckworth said. "Gatz is an idiot, but he wouldn't dare cross me after the tongue-lashing I gave him last night."

Fargo was in the saddle and reining the stallion toward the road before the words were out of the officer's mouth. "I'll catch up with you before you reach Fort Ripley," he pledged, jabbing his spurs lightly into the stallion.

Two soldiers near the road scampered out of the way as Fargo flew on by in a small cloud of dust. He slowed just long enough to check the tracks left by the Minnesota Militia. They had a two- to three-hour lead. He prayed that Wagon Annie had not unloaded the wagon the night before, that she had gotten a late start, and that she had not reached the main road yet.

He should have known better.

The Ovaro was winded and in need of a rest when Fargo drew to a stop abreast of the latticework that hid the secret trail. Only now the crude affair lay flat on the ground; many of its limbs were broken or mashed.

Tracks told the story. Wagon Annie had arrived at the thicket and shoved the latticework to one side so she could pass. At that moment, Major Mortimer Gatz and his company of Minnesota Militia had come around a bend to the north. There had been a confrontation, evidently, and a struggle. Two men had thrown Annie into the wagon bed and climbed onto the seat. Then the detail had gone on.

Fargo prodded the weary stallion. This was the last straw. Gatz had beaten him, had insulted him, and had been a thorn in his side ever since he reached Minnesota. He had put off tangling with the peacock long enough.

It was time for Major Mortimer Gatz to pay the piper.

8

It was another half an hour before Skye Fargo spotted tendrils of dust in the distance. He was holding the pinto to a trot so it would have enough strength left for a final sprint, if need be. In order to have the element of surprise, he left the road.

The rolling hills were thickly wooded, screening him from prying eyes. Fargo saw that the wagon was at the head of the column, with Gatz riding beside it. The militiamen were strung out in pairs, seated stiffly in their saddles as befitted the major's ideal of proper horsemanship.

Anne Standley's red hair was visible over the top of the wagon bed. Gatz appeared to be talking to her, and was gesturing grandly.

As soundlessly as the Sioux would do, Fargo passed the column without them being the wiser. Beyond the next sharp turn, he angled to the road and drew rein in the middle. Leaning down, he yanked the Henry from the saddle scabbard and fed a fresh cartridge into the chamber. Resting it across his saddle, he waited.

Soon the creaking of a wheel in need of grease and the plodding of the mules heralded the militiamen. Major Gatz had his attention on Wagon Annie, and did not see Fargo until the driver jerked on the reins and cried out, "Look there, sir!"

Mortimer Gatz stiffened, resentment blazing in his gaze. "You again! What are you doing here? Where's your good friend, Captain Beckworth?"

Fargo calmly kneed the Ovaro forward. The pair on the wagon seat were uncertain of what to do, and kept glancing at their superior for instructions. As for the rest of the company, they were out of sight around the bend and as yet had no idea what was going on. "I've come for Anne Standley," he said.

Wagon Annie stood up. Her wrists were tied behind her back, and she wore a tight gag. Over her left eye was a large bruise. During her struggle with the militiamen, her buckskin shirt had been torn at the shoulder, exposing her arm down to the elbow.

Fargo grinned at her. "Anyone ever mention that you're a mess in the morning?"

Gatz had turned his customary reddish hue. "What do you mean, you've come for her? This woman is in our custody, and I will brook no interference from the likes of you!"

Slowly raising the Henry, Fargo pointed it squarely at the major's chest. "I don't recall asking your permission. Cut her loose; then get back on your horse. You're coming with us."

"*What?*" Gatz bawled. "Who do you think you're talking to? At a word from me, you'll be cut to ribbons."

Fargo pulled back the hammer slowly so all of them heard it click. "Maybe so. But I'll get off at least one shot, and guess who takes the lead?"

Major Gatz's swelled chest deflated a few inches. "Now, hold on there, mister. You've just crossed the line. By openly threatening me, you are committing a criminal act. I now have the legal authority to take you into custody, just as we did this gun trafficker."

"What about the line you crossed the other night when you had your men jump me?" Fargo responded. "Who holds you to account for that?" He was passing the seat, and it was well that he did not take his eyes completely off the burly specimens on it, because the nearest one suddenly coiled and jumped, brawny fists upraised to bash him in the head.

Fargo was quicker. A short, powerful stroke of the Henry caught the militiaman in the midriff, upending the man in midair. The soldier's forehead cracked against the top of the front wheel, and he sprawled limply beside it, blood trickling from his split skin.

Both the other soldier and Major Gatz made stabs for their side arms, but Fargo swung the Henry up, forestalling them. "Shed the hardware, gents," he directed, "and do it carefully, or else."

The driver snatched his revolver out, and cast it into the weeds. Gatz hesitated, his features twisting in rabid hatred. For a moment Fargo thought the major would do something rash, but Gatz regained his self-control and flipped his pistol to the ground.

"You'll pay for this outrage, mister."

Two mounted troopers came around the bend and froze, gawking at Fargo. He stopped next to the officer. "Order the rest of your men to pull back a hundred yards."

"Like hell I will!"

Fargo jabbed the Henry into Gatz's ribs. "It's your life," he said. They locked eyes, and after a minute it was Gatz's will that broke. The proper commands were barked out. The pair nodded and disappeared. Seconds later the clatter of hooves assured Fargo that they had complied.

"I'll see that you hang for this," Gatz spat. "If it takes me the rest of my life, I will hunt you down and bring you to bay. If—"

Fargo had taken about all the guff he was going to. "If bluster was gold, you'd be the richest man in the country." He cut Gatz off. "Now, climb up in the wagon and do as I told you."

"Do it yourself, you son of a bitch."

The stock of the Henry streaked up and out. Mortimer Gatz was struck full in the face and catapulted from his mount as if smashed by a boulder. The soldier on the seat started to rise, but stopped when the Henry swiveled toward him.

Gatz flopped around like a chicken with its head chopped off, his hands over his mouth. Gurgling and groaning, he carried on as a five-year-old would until Fargo said, "On your feet. I didn't hit you any harder than you hit me the other night."

The major sat up. His lower lip was pulped, and he held a bloody tooth in his left palm. "No?" he blubbered in smoldering rage. "Look at what you've done! I can now add assaulting a duly constituted militia officer to the other charges that will be filed against you."

Fargo nodded at the freight wagon. "Annie, remember? And hurry it up before your men change their minds and try to be heroes."

The soldier on the seat swiveled around. "I'll untie her for you, sir," he told the officer, sliding a leg into the bed. "You stay there."

"No," Fargo said, and smiled grimly at Gatz. "I want *you* to do it."

If looks could kill, Fargo would have been reduced to a skeleton on the spot. Major Gatz rose, and went to throw the loose tooth away. Then he paused, stared at it, and stuck it into a pocket. Gripping the side of the wagon, he climbed up, awkwardly swinging his legs over the side. Wagon Annie turned so her back was to him, and he applied himself to the knots. She wrenched the gag off herself after her hands were free.

"Thanks, Skye," the redhead said, bestowing an affectionate glance at Fargo. "I tried to tell these idiots that I wasn't the one running repeaters to the Sioux, but they wouldn't listen."

"Climb on behind me and let's light a shuck," Fargo advised.

Wagon Annie stepped to the side, but stopped. "There's something I have to do first." With no hint of what she had in mind, she whirled, her right fist slamming into Mortimer

Gatz. The major staggered against the front seat, and would have fallen if the soldier there had not caught him. "That's for this," Annie said, touching the bruise over her eye. As fluidly as a panther, she vaulted from the wagon.

Gatz was holding his mouth again, his fingers stained red. He shrugged free of the soldier's grasp, straightened his saber's scabbard, and slid down. "I'll not forget that, woman," he said through clenched teeth.

"Don't you ever get tired of flapping your gums?" Wagon Annie said.

Fargo held out his hand and hoisted her up. Her arms looped around his waist, and she briefly rested her cheek on his shoulder. "Thank you," she said again, only softly this time so neither of the militiamen would hear. She gave his waist a gentle squeeze. "I'll have to find some way of paying you back."

Gatz was climbing onto his sorrel. His right boot missed the stirrup, and he had to bend to insert it. "I look forward to officiating at your hangings," he commented, wiping scarlet flecks from his lips with his sleeve. "It should draw large crowds."

"Shut up and ride," Fargo said, pointing due west. To the soldier on the seat, he added, "Tell the others not to follow us, if they know what is good for the major. I'll send him back unharmed once we're in the clear."

"You had better," the man said.

The Ovaro fell into step behind the sorrel. Gatz twisted frequently to glare, his mashed lip lending a demonical aspect to his already flinty countenance. Wagon Annie chuckled, her breath warm on Fargo's neck. "Some people never learn, do they? That man has too much acid in his system to ever enjoy life. He's only happy when he's hating."

Fargo checked their back trail every few minutes. Most of the militiamen were young and just foolhardy enough to ignore his warning. Should they call his bluff and give chase, he would flee rather than stand and fight. He had nothing against them personally, no desire to kill any. Most had joined the militia out of fear for the safety of the settlers. It was not their fault that their commander was unhinged.

They came to the game trail, and Fargo had Major Gatz take it to the northwest. For over an hour they wound deeper into virgin forest. Convinced that the militiamen had stayed put, Fargo reined up and directed the officer to do the same. "Now climb down," he said, "and start walking back."

Gatz balked. "But we must have covered four miles. You expect me to walk the entire way, through hostile territory, unarmed?"

"Why do you think I let you keep your sword?" Fargo rejoined. He helped Annie down, then dismounted himself to give the Ovaro a short breather.

Major Gatz had not budged. "I get it," he declared. "You're hoping that the Sioux will find me, or that a grizzly will pick up my scent. It's your way of disposing of me without pulling the trigger yourself."

Wagon Annie shook her head. "When the Good Lord passed out brains, you must have been in the outhouse. When will you get it through that thick head of yours that we're all on the same side. We don't want the Santees to be armed any more than you do."

"Spare me your lies," Gatz said. "With my own eyes I saw you sneak out of the trees this morning. What else were you doing back in the woods if not selling rifles to Fire Thunder's bunch?"

Wagon Annie clamped her lips together.

Fargo knew why the freighter did not want her secret known. He sympathized, but the time had come to lay all their cards on the table, as it were. "She takes food and clothes to the Sioux two or three times a year," he disclosed.

"Skye!" Annie cried, facing him. "What the hell did you do that for?"

"Would you rather it came out at a trial or a formal Army hearing?" Fargo challenged her.

"I'll lose my business if this jackass tells everyone!" Annie said. "Ed Wallace will finally get his wish and have Minnesota all to himself."

Mortimer Gatz was glancing from one of them to the other. "You're serious?" he said. "She really does aid and abet the enemy?"

Annie wheeled on him like a female hawk about to rip into prey. "Since when is giving food to the Indians a crime? They have to eat, just like we do. And half the time they can't, since crooked storekeepers and government agents cheat them out of the money the government sends to feed them."

Gatz made the mistake of shrugging and saying, "So what if a few savages go hungry? Sooner or later we'll have to exterminate every last one of them anyway."

In a bound Annie reached him and yanked him off the sorrel. She flew into him with feet and fists, the major trying with limited success to ward off the rain of blows. Fargo grabbed her and pulled her back, having to duck when she tried to box his ear.

"Let me go! He has it coming!" Annie fumed. She lashed a foot at Gatz's cheek that narrowly missed. "He's scum, pure and simple!"

Gatz did not know when to leave well enough alone. "Me? You're the one treating heathens as if they were normal people. What have the stinking Sioux ever done for our kind but give us grief?"

Annie quieted. In an icy tone, she said, "I'll tell you what they've done." She paused, her arms dropping, and Fargo let go. "Five years ago we had the worst winter ever. Do you remember?"

"Sure," Gatz said, rising. "It snowed in late October, and we didn't see grass again until April. The temperature was below freezing most of the time, so the Mississippi nearly froze over."

"Hardly anyone could get in or out of Minneapolis, the road was so choked with snow," Annie said. "In January we had five feet of it fall in twenty-four hours."

"So?" Gatz replied. "What does the weather have to do with anything?"

"Just this. The garrison at Fort Ripley ran low on supplies. They needed more or they would starve. But no one could get through to them. Wallace sent a few of his boys, and they got stuck. So Colonel Williams begged me to try. And I did." Annie's gaze seemed to turn inward, and she shivered as if cold. "I was cocky in those days, even more than I am now. I thought I could do anything. So I headed out one morning, and got as far as Grizzly Heights when another storm struck. Before I knew it, my wagon was half buried."

Fargo had been caught in a few blizzards in his time, and he hoped he never was again. Nature was an unforgiving taskmaster at the best of times. Blizzards and tornadoes and the like were her temper tantrums, certain death for the unwary.

Annie coughed. "I crawled under the wagon and covered myself with blankets, but that still didn't keep out the cold. So I gathered what little wood I could to start a small fire. By then my fingers were half-frozen, and I couldn't get a flame going. Little by little, I was freezing alive."

"I still don't see your point," Major Gatz said.

"You will. Because just when the last of my strength left me and I laid down to die, four Sioux warriors out hunting found my wagon and dug me out. They took me to their village, where one of them had me put in his lodge. His wife and daughters tended me day and night for two days, keeping me warm and forcing soup down my throat. They saved my life."

Gatz was unimpressed. "One act of compassion does not qualify them for sainthood. I'd wager they had an ulterior motive."

"You'd lose the bet," Wagon Annie said. "They never

asked for anything in return, never touched the canned goods and flour in my wagon even though they were starving themselves." She inhaled, then straightened. "The warrior who saved me was Red Wing. Ever since, I've done all I can to repay him and his people, and that includes feeding them out of my own pocket."

"You've done the right thing," Fargo complimented her. Many whites would have taken the Sioux's help for granted and gone on with their lives, not caring one whit what happened to their benefactors.

The major was rubbing his jaw, his brow furrowed as if he were pondering her revelation. Fargo could have told her that she was wasting her breath, as Gatz's next statement confirmed. "I'm inclined to believe you are telling the truth, Miss Standley, but that doesn't alter the fact that you have been providing food and goods to savages who have vowed to drive all whites from their territory."

"Is what I've done against the law?" Annie asked testily, her anger surging once more.

"No, not yet, but it should be," Gatz said. "The sooner bleeding hearts like you realize that the Sioux are our enemies, the sooner we can dispose of them and get on with the divine task of spreading our culture across North America. Surely, you've heard of our Manifest Destiny?"

Fargo had heard the term before. There were those in positions of power in the U.S. government who believed that it was America's God-given right to rule all the land between the Atlantic and the Pacific. If that meant wiping out every last Indian in the process, so be it.

"I should have known you would believe in that hogwash," Wagon Annie said. With a gesture of contempt, she turned away from the officer. "Skye, get me out of here before I do something we'll both regret."

"Mount up," Fargo instructed her, and forked leather himself. The stallion needed more rest, but they had to put more distance between them and the militia patrol.

Major Gatz watched them ride off, his hand on his saber.

"I meant what I said about hunting you down," he hollered. "From now on you'll never have a moment's peace. Every minute of every day you'll be looking over your shoulder."

Wagon Annie cursed, then said to Fargo, "The man never shuts up, does he? I swear, he must be in love with the sound of his own voice."

"I've met people like that," Fargo remarked. Thankfully, they were soon too far off to hear the fanatic shout. When Fargo glanced back for the last time before entering dense pines, Gatz had not moved. The man just stood there, staring after them accusingly.

"So what now, handsome?" Annie asked as the foliage closed around them. "I've never been a fugitive before. Should we head for California? Maybe change our names when we get there and open a bakery?"

"Nothing so drastic," Fargo said, grinning. He reined the stallion to the northeast. It was his plan to rejoin Captain Beckworth, explain everything, and rely on his friend to safely escort Wagon Annie back to Fort Snelling. An appeal to Colonel Williams should prove fruitful. The colonel liked Annie and was bound to put Gatz in his place.

They covered the better part of a mile when Annie suddenly exclaimed, "Goodness gracious! I almost forgot!" Twisting, she opened one of the major's saddlebags and removed her coiled bullwhip. "That high-handed weasel stuffed Precious in here after his men pinned me on the ground."

It reminded Fargo of a question he had been meaning to ask. "Why did you give your whip a name?"

"Why shouldn't I? I knew a blacksmith once who named his favorite hammer. And a cousin of mine called her sled 'George' after her boyfriend." Annie patted the whip. "Precious is a fitting handle. It's gotten me out of more scrapes than I care to mention. Saved my hide a dozen times. So you might say this whip is as precious to me as life itself."

The sun was directly overhead when Fargo called a halt on the grassy bank of a bubbling stream. He had been pushing the Ovaro for hours, and the trusty stallion was beginning to flag. Unsaddling, he let the pinto drink to its heart's content while he sat and leaned back against a boulder, the Henry in his lap.

Wagon Annie moved off a dozen yards, and practiced with her whip a spell. She beamed every time she made the lash crack like a gunshot. About the tenth or eleventh swing, she said, "This is what I'd like to do to that jackass, Gatz!" and sent the whip sizzling toward a dead branch on an oak tree. The branch split with a loud *crack*.

North of the bank was a pool created by a tree that had fallen across the stream some time ago, partially stemming the flow. Coiling her whip, the redhead walked over to it. "Look at how clear that water is," she commented. "And I haven't had a bath in days."

"Go ahead," Fargo prompted. "I'll stand guard."

"Why not join me?"

Fargo thought she was joking until he saw the hungry look she gave him. "With the Minnesota Militia on our trail and Fire Thunder somewhere in the area? You believe in living dangerously."

"No, I believe in living life to the fullest," Annie said. "I learned long ago that when I want something, I have to reach out and take it. It's the only way a woman can compete with men in a man's world."

Dropping the whip, the redhead began to shuck her clothes. Her hat fell first, and she gave her gorgeous long mane a shake, spilling red curls over her shoulders. Her boots were peeled off one at a time. Standing, she deliberately faced Fargo and boldly shed her buckskin shirt.

Her body was magnificent. Her skin glistened with vitality, her arms more muscular than those of most women. Wide shoulders tapered to a thin waist. Full, ripe breasts swayed as she bent to take off her pants, her nipples jutting from rosy aureoles. When her pants fell to her ankles, she kicked them off in his direction. Her legs were sturdy yet trim, as befitted someone who worked outdoors and daily did a lot of heavy lifting.

Placing her slender hands on her full hips, Wagon Annie regarded Fargo with twin twinkles in her lustrous eyes. She displayed no shame, no embarrassment. Wearing only an impish grin, she seductively ran a hand from her neck to her navel, passing between her breasts. The thatch of red hair at the junction of her thighs moved in a circular pattern as she playfully pumped her hips.

Fargo's mouth was so dry that he could barely swallow. A constriction in his throat grew worse when she cocked a finger at him. Right then he would not have cared if the whole Minnesota Militia and the entire Santee tribe combined came swooping down on them.

"What about it, handsome? Are you going to sit there like a bump on a log all day, or are you the man I think you are?"

What man could resist such an invitation?

9

Skye Fargo was only human. His common sense told him to stay where he was and keep watch. But the dazzling sight of Anne Standley's sleek naked figure as she gracefully spun, stepped to the edge of the bank, and dived neatly into the pool, was too enticing to resist. Giving the woods a cursory scan, he rose and walked to the pool.

Wagon Annie was a fabulous swimmer. She cleaved the water with smooth, powerful strokes to the opposite side, then did an acrobatic flip underwater and propelled herself back toward him by pushing off from the side. Her red mane poked above the surface, and she laughed merrily.

"I'm waiting, big man!"

Fargo undressed swiftly, placing the Henry and his gun belt as close to the stream as practical in case they were needed. Moving to a flat spot, he extended both arms and performed a long, arcing dive. Cold water enveloped him like a knife sheath. He broke out in goose bumps as he swam to the top and lowered his legs.

The pool was waist deep, the bottom covered with smooth, mostly circular stones. They were so slick that Fargo had to walk gingerly in order not to slip. As he turned toward the east bank, a willowy form surged underwater toward his legs.

Smiling broadly, Wagon Annie surfaced and brazenly admired his muscular body from head to toe. She stood within arm's reach, a vision of beauty if ever there was one. Her soaked hair clung to her neck and shoulders, the bright red strands accenting her smooth facial features and complementing her equally red, full lips. Glistening drops of water rolled down over her full bosom, across the flat of her stomach, to the red triangle below. She gave her head a shake, her hair spraying him with moisture. "Come on, handsome," she said. "Let's have some fun."

Annie dived, and Fargo followed. She was an excellent swimmer. It was all he could do to keep up with her as she flashed along the stream bottom, changing direction on a moment's notice, her taunting smile luring him on.

Frolicking like a pair of otters, they swam for over fifteen minutes, back and forth and up and down, crisscrossing the pool again and again. Gradually, they grew closer. Annie's body often brushed his, her legs touching his when they turned, or her breasts sliding across his chest when they were face-to-face.

Fargo could not help being aroused. His manhood, predictably, soon resembled a flagpole. The redhead noticed, and once, when they came up for air, she stared at his member and hungrily licked her lips. Then she dived once more, beckoning him to join in her sensual watery ballet.

On the east side of the stream, to the left of where Fargo had placed the Henry and his gun belt, was a grassy spot at the base of the bank. Annie swam to it, clambered out, and sat breathing heavily. "That was refreshing," she commented as he came out of the water on his hands and knees and sank onto his side beside her.

"We should get dressed. Gatz might show up," Fargo told her. He only said it because it was the logical thing to do, the safe thing to do. But he no more wanted to get dressed than he wanted to walk barefoot across a burning bed of coals. He gazed at the swell of her ripe breasts, his mouth watering in anticipation.

"You don't fool me," Wagon Annie said. Bending, she wrapped her hand around his pole. "This is what you really want to do. Am I right?"

Fargo's answer was to reach up and pull her facedown to

his. Her lips were aflame. They mashed against his as if she were trying to devour him alive. Her tongue thrust them apart, speared into his mouth, and entwined with his in a silken dance that mimicked their frolic in the water. She was an incredible kisser.

Annie leaned against him, her globes pressing into his chest, her nipples firm and growing harder by the second. She lightly stroked his organ, her fingernails swirling from side to side. At the bottom she cupped him and massaged. The sensation was so exquisite that Fargo nearly exploded right then and there.

Running a hand up her back, Fargo brought it around in front and slipped it between them. Her breast filled his palm, and then some. Kneading it gently, he provoked a throaty growl that grew louder when he lowered his mouth to her other nipple and tweaked it with his teeth.

Annie abruptly pushed him back onto the grass. Grasping his hips, she wriggled on top of him. Like a woman possessed, she ran her hands over every square inch of his body that she could reach. Her lips wrapped around his tongue, and she sucked on it, drawing it into her mouth.

Fargo continued to press the flesh of her right breast. Her hips bumped against his in a hint of the frenzied coupling to come. She acted as if she were starved for male companionship, and maybe she was. Strong, tough women like Annie were apt to scare off most men.

She broke their embrace to slide slowly downward, delivering tiny kisses to his chest and stomach. Fargo placed his hands on both sides of her head as her mouth dipped even farther, and a moist feeling engulfed his throbbing manhood. She nibbled and lathered him until he was afraid he could not take any more.

Pulling her up beside him, Fargo covered both of her wonderful mounds with his hands and applied his mouth to her earlobe. It stimulated her into cooing and moaning and rubbing her legs against his. They parted when he lowered a hand to her nether mound.

"Yes, yes, yes," Wagon Annie breathed.

She was an oven down there, a cauldron of brewing lust so moist and hot that Fargo's finger glided into her tunnel as easily as into a bowl of honey. At the contact her spine arched, and she hissed like a cat.

"More! More!"

Fargo was eager to oblige. Sliding down between her legs, he applied his mouth to her nether lips. It was the trigger that unleashed a human volcano. Annie hooked her legs over his shoulders, grasped the back of his head, and bucked into him with vigor and vim. Groaning and grunting, she pushed his face deeper, her thighs opening and closing against his head, her heels gouging into his shoulder blades. Half her thrusts lifted him partway off the grass.

Fargo licked and probed until his tongue was so sore, he was half sure it would fall out. He tried to pull back, but Annie was not satisfied yet. She ground him against her womanhood, insisting without words that he keep going, so he did. His cheeks and chin were drenched when at last she sank back in partial exhaustion, permitting him to rise.

Spreading her legs farther, Fargo positioned himself on his knees, applied the tip of his pole to her slit, and, just for the heck of it, rammed into her to the hilt. Annie cried out, then sagged, momentarily limp, her eyes glazed with passion, her lips trembling. Suddenly rousing to life, she wrapped her arms around his shoulders and drove up into him as if to fling both of them into the stream.

Annie became a human bucking bronco. She thrust up to match his own pumping hips, their mutual motion rocking them in heated embrace, her mouth glued to his. Fargo lost track of time, of his surroundings, of everything except for the ecstasy that coursed through his body, the ecstasy to which he was as addicted as some men were to alcohol and opium. He could never, ever get enough.

They were locked for what seemed like forever in the throes of supreme delight. Then Wagon Annie stiffened, her whole body shook, and she called out, "Now! Oh,

Skye! Now!" Fargo pounded into her with a vengeance, his own long delayed explosion rising to the critical point. When the climax came, the sky spun and danced, his breath catching in his throat. A bolt of lightning shot up and down his backbone. His hips churned in a frenzy that gradually tapered as he expended the last of his energy and sank on top of her, cushioned by her heaving bosom.

For the longest while neither of them spoke. Annie entwined her fingers in his hair and kept chuckling softly to herself. Fargo was content to rest, to savor a fleeting feeling of peace with the world.

"I liked that, handsome." Annie broke the silence.

"No fooling?" Fargo joshed sleepily.

Rather anxiously, she asked, "You don't aim to stick around these parts very long, do you?"

"No," Fargo admitted.

Annie fell quiet again for a while. "Too bad," she sighed. "We could have us some grand old times." She tweaked his ear. "You'll be sorry if you go. The right woman can make a man's life more worth living, if you know what I mean."

"I do," Fargo said, wishing she had not brought it up. Most women inevitably did, though. Quite naturally, when they found a man they were fond of and who aroused them to a degree they had rarely been aroused, they wanted to hang onto him. The problem was that Fargo had no intention of settling down any time soon—if ever.

As if privy to his thoughts, Wagon Annie said, "I'm sorry. I shouldn't have brought it up. It's not as if you've tried to deceive me, like some men do."

Tricking a woman into making love was something Fargo had never done, and never would. He knew some men who had, of course, men who pledged undying love and fawned over a female until she believed their lies and went to bed with them. Nine times out of ten, once the scoundrels got what they were after, they'd light out as if their feet were on fire in search of greener pastures.

"After I've helped the Army corral Fire Thunder, I'll be leaving," Fargo confided.

Annie ran a finger along his shoulder. "Can't you stick around just a little while, lover?"

Fargo looked up. Her devilish grin was more than he could resist. "A little while wouldn't hurt," he responded, and they both laughed.

Their mirth dissolved when the Ovaro let out with a low whinny. Fargo was on his feet before the nicker died, tugging on his clothes. Long familiarity with every sound his horse made told him that the stallion had caught sight or the scent of someone or something that he should know about.

"What is it?" Wagon Annie asked, sitting up.

"Get dressed," Fargo instructed her. Scooping up his gun belt and the Henry, he ran to where the pinto and the sorrel were staring to the south. At first he saw nothing out of the ordinary. Movement on a barren knob alerted him to a column of riders in brown uniforms. At their head rode a wide-shouldered man whose uniform glistened with silver trappings.

"Damn," Fargo said, and rushed to their saddles. The Minnesota Militiamen were no more than a quarter of a mile away. He did not have any time to spare.

Wagon Annie hustled over, her shirt hanging out, her hat lopsided, her boots in hand. The bullwhip was coiled over her left shoulder. "What's the rush?" she inquired, scouring the woodland. "I don't see anything."

"Gatz," Fargo said.

The redhead swore like a trooper, adding, "I didn't think he could find his own backside without a diagram. How do you reckon he found us?"

"One of his men must be a tracker," Fargo guessed. Either that, or it had been sheer dumb luck. The moment he had the Ovaro saddled, he assisted Annie with the sorrel. Mounted, they crossed the stream. It would do no good to try and mask their tracks by riding north in the middle.

They would muddy the water so badly that it would be obvious.

Side by side they scaled a hill to a shelf. By now the militia patrol was only a few hundred yards from the pool. A skinny soldier rode in front of Gatz, head bent low to see the ground.

"You were right," Annie said.

Reining around, Fargo trotted northward. The Ovaro and the sorrel had rested sufficiently long that they could go for hours without stopping. Which was good, because he chose the roughest terrain, traversing rocky slopes and penetrating thick stands of pines and brush.

"So much for feeling clean," Wagon Annie remarked after they had been on the go for over an hour. Mopping her brow, she said, "I could use another dunk in that stream."

A spiny ridge offered the vantage site Fargo wanted. Stopping, he rose in the stirrups and pulled his hat brim low to ward off the glare of brilliant sunshine. From their elevation the woodland canopy resembled an unbroken sea of green. Unbroken, that was, except for the blue ribbon of the stream and scattered clearings.

"Surely, we've lost them," Annie said.

The next moment a string of riders appeared, crossing a clearing half a mile away. "No such luck," Fargo said, impressed by the militia tracker. Whoever the man was, he was better than most. "Come on."

On the other side of the ridge lay a verdant winding valley that brought them to another series of hills dotted with small lakes. Fargo did his best to disguise their trail. Three times he climbed down to brush out their tracks or to cover them with leaves and fallen limbs.

About four in the afternoon Fargo drew rein on a flat-topped hill, one of the highest in their vicinity. Squatting on a rocky knob, he surveyed the countryside they had passed through. If the patrol was still after them, they were in trouble.

"Look at what I just found in Gatz's saddlebags," Wagon Annie said, hunkering next to him and holding out a brass spyglass. "There's a whole bunch of other stuff in there. A compass, ammunition, spare shirts, a folding knife, and a bottle of patent medicine for warts."

Fargo unfolded the telescope and peered through it. He concentrated on gaps in the trees, but saw no evidence of pursuit. Fixing the spyglass on a meadow they had crossed over an hour ago, he watched for a while. When no one appeared, he began to shift to the right. At that instant the head of the militia column rode into view, the same tracker leaning from the saddle as before. "Did you say there were shirts in Gatz's saddlebag?" he asked.

"Yes. Why?"

"Fetch them." Fargo folded the spyglass, slid it into a pocket, then drew the Arkansas toothpick and tested the twin-edged blade on a stem of grass he plucked out. The knife sheared neatly through it.

Wagon Annie hurried back. "Here you go," she said, dumping a pair of folded brown shirts beside him. Both were adorned with silver trim and braids. "What are you up to, handsome?"

"We haven't shaken them yet," Fargo said while spreading the shirts flat. Unbuttoning both, he cut off their sleeves at the shoulders. Next he sliced each shirt down the middle of the back, which left him with four halves. He needed eight pieces, four for each horse, so he slit the fabric down the center again. The sleeves he trimmed, ending up with eight roughly equal strips.

Annie did not comprehend until Fargo took one of the large pieces and one of the strips, and knelt in front of the Ovaro. Lifting the stallion's right front leg, he wrapped the wide piece over the hoof and tied it in place with the strip.

"I never heard of this trick before," the redhead commented. "It will hide our tracks, won't it?"

"That's the idea," Fargo said. "I learned it from an old

Comanche. They're some of the best horse thieves in the world."

"They live down Texas way, as I recollect," Annie said. "My, but you do get around."

"If you only knew."

In short order Fargo had tied material over the hooves of both horses. It would not quite erase all evidence of their passage, but it would keep the sharp edges of the hooves from digging as deeply into the soil as they would otherwise. By sticking to the hardest ground he could find, he'd make it much more difficult for the militia tracker to stay on their trail.

"Let's ride," Fargo said, grabbing the saddle horn and levering his body into the saddle. He maintained a canter for the first few miles, slowing afterward, since by then only an hour or so of daylight remained and there was no possibility the patrol would overtake them before nightfall.

All was going reasonably well. Fargo had high hopes of shaking Gatz and reaching Fort Ripley by the evening of the next day. He should have known it would not be that easy.

"Skye," Wagon Annie declared. "My horse stumbled on some loose rocks awhile back and has been acting up ever since. I think it's going lame."

Fargo shifted. The sorrel was favoring its left front leg, and would limp every few strides. Immediately, they reined up. The piece of shirt was still in place, so that could not be the cause. He removed the strip and ran his fingers over the animal's limb from the fetlock to the elbow. The knee was terribly swollen, but he found no apparent damage to the tendons, muscles, or bone.

"A good, long rest might be all it needs," Fargo said, based on stricken horses he had seen before that made dramatic overnight recoveries after being nearly ridden to death. Since it was unwise to ride the animal much farther, Fargo rose and scanned the tableland spread out before them. Rife with balsam fir, aspens, and white spruce, it included isolated rocky areas as well as extensive patches of wintergreen.

Leading their mounts, Fargo and Wagon Annie walked to a tangle of man-size boulders. An open space shielded on three sides was as likely a place as any to spend the night.

"We can have a small fire," Fargo proposed. "You get it going while I try to rustle up something for our supper."

Wagon Annie was taking off the sorrel's saddle. "Hold on," she said. "Why risk the shot being heard when we can eat courtesy of Major Gatz?" From the bottom of one of the saddlebags she lifted a rarity on the frontier: two small cans of peaches. Also a folding knife. "Our raving bigot has a sweet tooth."

So it was coffee and peaches for their meal, Fargo spearing his with the toothpick, Annie using her fingers and smacking her lips with every other bite. When she downed the last one, she upended the can over her mouth, the thick syrup oozing over her cheeks and jaw. She wiped it off with the back of her hand, licked her fingers clean, and leaned back, contented.

"I haven't had any of those in a coon's age. Who can afford them, as pricey as they are?"

Fargo leaned back on his saddle and glanced westward at the sinking sun. It would not be long before the predators that roamed at night were abroad. As proof, a lone wolf had appeared on a knoll sixty yards away. He dismissed it as unimportant. Wolves were common in the north country and seldom posed a threat to humans.

"I'm feeling awfully tired," Wagon Annie said, stretching languidly. She winked and smirked. "Can't imagine why, can you?"

Fargo was feeling the effects of their long ride and their escapade at the stream himself. He had to stay awake, though, long enough to verify that the Minnesota Militia had given up. Yawning, he looked westward.

Three wolves had appeared.

The redhead had grown somber. "If by some miracle I get out of this mess alive, my days in Minneapolis are numbered. Once Gatz spreads his lies, hardly anyone will give me the time of day."

"You never know," Fargo said absently, his eyelids leaden. To combat his fatigue, he poured himself another cup of steaming hot coffee.

"It isn't fair," Annie chattered on. "I've worked my hind end to the bone to make something of myself, to build up my freight company to where I can compete with the big boys; and now the biggest of all will take over my routes because I tried to do the right thing by the Santees."

Fargo sipped and noticed a flock of ducks winging to the northwest. Following them with his eyes, he discovered that five wolves now paced the crest of the knoll. It was a small pack, as packs went, and they were probably merely curious. He added a limb to the fire.

Annie had gone on talking, more to herself than to him. "You have no notion of what it's like to be a woman nowadays. Men are always trying to put me in what they call my proper place, as if my being in business for myself isn't ladylike. They look down their noses at me because of how I dress and act. Then, almost in the same breath, they have the gall to ogle my body as if I were a slab of meat up for sale."

"I'd say you have cause to be proud of what you've done with your life," Fargo remarked. "Who cares what anyone else thinks?"

The redhead smiled. "Thank you. Major Gatz and his ilk wouldn't agree, though. His kind want all us females to spend our days bent over hot stoves and washtubs."

The Ovaro was staring toward the knoll. Fargo did likewise, and was mildly surprised to see eight or nine wolves milling about. It was a bigger pack than he had figured.

"Funny thing is," Wagon Annie said, "if I ever get me a husband and a passel of kids, I'll be the best darned wife and mother any woman has ever been. I'll cook and wash until I'm sick of it, but it will be my choice. I'll do it because I care for my family, not because someone forces me to—"

Fargo stopped listening. A guttural yip snapped his head around, and he leaped to his feet in astonishment. Pouring over the knoll were fifteen or twenty wolves, with more appearing every second.

The pack made straight for the boulders.

10

Skye Fargo had never seen so many wolves in one place at one time. Large packs of ten or twelve were common on the plains, where they shadowed buffalo herds, thinning out the aged and the infirm. A pack of this size, though, over twenty-five strong, was extraordinary. Grabbing the Henry, he took a hasty bead on one of the fleetest but did not shoot. The scent of blood might provoke the rest into a concerted attack.

"Skye, what is it?" Wagon Annie asked, jumping up and grasping her bullwhip. She looked past him, blurting, "Land sakes! Shouldn't we make a run for it?"

"No," Fargo said, basing his decision on his knowledge of wild beasts.

Once, years ago, Fargo had seen a mountain lion stalk a herd of six deer. The does spotted the big cat well before it reached them, and for long moments the cougar and its quarry had stared at one another. Then one of the deer bolted. Instantly, the lion had gone after it, passing within a few feet of the other deer without harming them. That incident, and many others, had convinced Fargo the surest way to incite a predator into attacking was to flee.

The onrushing wolves spooked the sorrel. Uttering a high-pitched whinny, it pulled at the rope tether. Fargo dashed over to keep the horse from running off. His own stallion showed no fright. It had its ears pricked and was tensed to resist if set upon.

Like a rippling gray stream, the wolves flowed toward

them. He raised the Henry, but just when he was about to shoot and drop the leader in the slim hope that the rest would run off, the gray stream parted, about half veering to the right, the rest to the left. In moments the cluster of boulders was ringed by four-legged specters who padded back and forth or stood growling and snarling.

Wagon Annie held her bullwhip ready to flick. "What do they want, Skye? Why are they acting like this?"

Fargo did not know. It was not unusual for wolves to approach campfires, more out of curiosity than anything else. It had happened to him many times during his travels. But this pack acted more hostile than most. A few of the bigger wolves were so close to the boulders that he could see their teeth gleam in the firelight.

"Shoot your gun," Annie suggested. "Maybe that will scare them off."

"It could also goad them into attacking," Fargo pointed out. He'd much rather let the pack make the first move. The wolves might just run off without causing any trouble.

"There's one way to find out," Wagon Annie said. Before he could stop her, she pivoted and swung her whip at a wolf in front of a small boulder near her. The lash cracked like a gunshot. Yowling, the wolf leaped back to escape a second swing, and Annie laughed. "I'm not about to let this bunch of mangy critters buffalo me!"

A few of the wolves retreated, but the majority, some hunched forward as if about to spring, edged toward the boulders. One of the largest, whose bristling chest sported a white blaze, snarled fiercely and focused exclusively on the redhead.

Fargo turned to shoot it. Suddenly, the sorrel reared, nickering in rising terror. He had his hands full holding on, so there was nothing he could do when the pack leader vaulted onto a boulder and coiled to leap at Anne.

The bullwhip whistled shrilly, the lash catching the wolf between the eyes. Hair and blood flew every which way. Tossing its head in agony, the wolf sprang backward.

"That ought to teach these varmints!" Annie gloated.

But it didn't. The pack reformed, a wedge of growling gray moving toward her. Fargo was holding onto the bucking sorrel with one hand and trying to level the Henry with the other. It was hopeless.

Whinnying louder than ever, the sorrel tore loose and bolted. It sailed over the protective ring of boulders, landing among the wolves preparing to rush Annie. Immediately, the predators pounced, biting and snapping and tearing at its legs. The sorrel kicked and plunged, fighting to break free.

"We have to help it!" Wagon Annie cried, rushing to the boulders and laying about her to the right and left, the crack-crack-crack of the whip barely audible above the bedlam of slavering wolves and the whinnies of the panic-stricken horse.

So far none of the pack had gone after the Ovaro, but Fargo knew that once they brought the sorrel down, as they surely would, and once the scent of blood aroused their lust to kill, they would swarm into the circle to get at the stallion—and Annie and him. Consequently, he ran to the redhead's side and began working the repeater just as fast as he could pump the lever. Five, six, seven shots smashed into the whirlwind of fur and hooves. Five wolves died, twitching and convulsing. Most of the rest promptly scattered.

Most, but not all. Seven refused to be run off, among them the big male with the blaze on its chest. Body slung low to the ground, it streaked toward Fargo and Annie. He barely had time to fix the front bead on the white blaze and stroke the trigger. The stock bucked into his shoulder. The booming retort rolled off across the tableland, over the body of the downed wolf as it jerked and flopped about.

The last six fled. Howling and growling, they vanished into the darkness with their hairy brethren.

"We did it!" Wagon Annie declared.

She spoke too soon. Because the sorrel took a single faltering step, then keeled over, rolling onto its right side and whinnying pitiably.

"Stay put!" Fargo directed Annie in case the pack should return. Clearing the boulders, he darted to the horse. Enough light from the fire reached it to reveal that two of its legs had virtually been chewed to ribbons and that its throat had been torn open. Blood gushed, already forming a pool that spread rapidly as Fargo looked on.

The sorrel would die a horrible, lingering death unless Fargo did something. Touching the muzzle to its forehead, he saw the animal look up at him, saw the torment and fear it was enduring. He fired once more.

Wagon Annie bounded onto a boulder and shook her whip at the departing pack. "Damn you vermin all to hell! Come back here so we can kill more of you!"

Fargo backed to the boulders. Off in the night a few skulking forms were visible, stragglers who no doubt intended to sneak in later for a bite of horse flesh. They posed no threat so long as there were only three or four.

"I never have been fond of wolves," Annie commented. "Bunch of oversize coyotes is all they are." She stared sadly at the sorrel. "Reminds me of when I was ten and a wolf killed a colt of mine. I was a gentle soul back then, but if I'd caught it, I would have strangled it with my bare hands."

Fargo was thinking of the Ovaro. They had to ride double now, and they had thirty miles of rough countryside to cover before they reached Fort Ripley.

"Life sure ain't fair, is it?" Wagon Annie said, more to herself than to him. "What did that poor sorrel ever do to deserve to die like that?" She added more wood to the fire, the flames blazing higher. "In case those devils take it into their heads to come back," she said when he glanced around.

Fargo doubted they would, but he let her do it. "You can turn in first," he said. "I'll keep watch."

Annie looked at him as if he were insane. "Do you really expect me to sleep with all those wolves out there?"

"Most have run off," Fargo told her. "They won't bother us anymore."

As if to prove him a liar, a wolf gave voice to a long, wavering howl. It was answered by another, then another, and soon a throaty lupine chorus serenaded them on all sides. Fargo reloaded the Henry, loosened the Colt in its holster, and sat with his back to the fire so the glare would not limit his vision.

Wagon Annie pulled Gatz's saddle over beside his, and took a seat. "I never heard so many at one time before," she remarked. "My grandpa used to say that back in his day, the wolves were as thick as fleas and were forever killing livestock and such. This must be what it was like."

At one time, Fargo knew, wolves had been as thick east of the Mississippi River as they now were west of it. As settlements grew, their numbers had steadily dwindled. High bounties posted for their hides had a lot to do with it. So many had been slain that in some states they had been completely wiped out.

It didn't surprise Fargo none. Any animal that posed a nuisance or could earn people money never survived very long. The same thing had nearly happened to the beaver up in the high country. If not for the collapse of the beaver market when silk came along, fur trappers would have exterminated the species in their quest for prime peltries.

Now some were saying the same would happen to the buffalo one day. Fargo couldn't see how, when there were millions and millions of the huge dumb brutes. But it troubled him that there was talk back East about wiping the great herds out in order to destroy the Indian tribes, whose land some whites coveted.

A gray streak materialized, racing out of the gloom to the sorrel. A quick snap of powerful jaws, and the wolf sped off with a large, juicy morsel clamped in its mouth.

"You should have shot it," Annie said.

"Why waste the ammo?" Fargo responded. Besides, the sorrel was dead. It would only lie there, and slowly rot or be consumed by scavengers.

"I wonder what that pesky major did with my wagon?" Annie said out of the blue.

"He only has ten men with him now," Fargo mentioned. "My guess is that he had the other two stay with it, or take it back to Minneapolis."

"Lord, I hope they didn't go to town. They'll spread the word, and if I ever show my face there again, I'm liable to be lynched on sight."

Fargo squeezed her shoulder. "I wouldn't let that happen. Neither would Captain Beckworth or the colonel."

Annie took off her hat and wedged it onto her left knee. "Have you ever gone up against a lynch mob before? It would take all the troops at Fort Snelling to keep me alive. I'd have to sell my freight office for what little I could get, and leave the territory under armed escort."

Another phantom form flashed out of nowhere to tear off a hunk of bloody meat.

"I can't stand to watch," Annie said. Rolling onto her side and curling into a ball, she covered her face with her hat. "Maybe I will try to get some sleep, after all. Wake me when it's my turn."

Fargo rested a hand on her arm. She was deeply depressed, and he couldn't blame her. Everything seemed to be going against her of late. The threat of losing the business she had worked so hard to make a success must be the worst blow of all. He wished there were something he could do to bolster her spirits.

Another wolf helped itself to a piece of the sorrel. The success of the first three inspired others. Soon one wolf after another flashed out of the night, tore greedily at the carcass, then sped away triumphant. The whole time, other members of the pack continued with their hair-raising refrain.

"Infernal critters," Wagon Annie muttered sleepily.

Fargo saw a wolf slinking toward them instead of the dead horse. Twisting, he plucked a small burning brand from the fire and hurled it over the boulders. It had the desired result. The wolf spun and vanished in the blink of an eye.

After that, none of the pack came anywhere near the camp. They were content to feast on the quarry they had already brought down. Some, more bold than the rest, sprawled across the sorrel and ate at a leisurely pace. The crunch of their teeth on bone and the rending of flesh, combined with the red glare of their eyes in the firelight, was enough to scare most men silly, but Fargo was too accustomed to the ways of the wild for it to have any effect on him.

Wagon Annie must have been more tired than she let on, because within twenty minutes of lying down, she was snoring lightly.

Fargo figured he would let her sleep until the wee hours of the morning. He was tired himself, but she needed the rest more.

Midnight came and went, and still the wolves would not leave. By then two thirds of the sorrel was gone, and they took to fighting among themselves over the remainder. Fargo was witness to a fight between two husky males over the same portion of flank. They tumbled about, snarling and snapping, until the loser slunk off with his tail between his legs.

Little by little Fargo's eyelids grew heavy. It became a battle for him to stay awake. He tried every trick he knew of, shaking his head and slapping himself, getting up every now and then to add wood to the fire, and pacing in a circle. Early on, he brought the pinto closer to the fire, just to be safe.

Years of practice enabled Fargo to tell the time by the stars. The Big Dipper was at its three o'clock position when he dozed off for a minute without meaning to do so. It startled him. He snapped awake, staring at the wolves, glad none had noticed his lapse.

Sometime between four and five, the pack began to drift off in twos and threes. Daylight was not far off, and they were going to hole up. After the last one blended into the murky woods, Fargo allowed himself to relax. He could afford to take a short nap before the sun rose.

It could not have been more than ten or fifteen minutes after he fell asleep that the Ovaro nickered softly. Fargo came half awake, his sluggish senses balking, his body craving more rest. He blinked, forcing himself to wake up. That nicker had been the kind the stallion uttered when it wanted to warn him of imminent danger.

Something cold and hard gouged into Fargo's temple. Every lingering vestige of sleep was gone. He grew instantly, fully alert.

"Don't so much as twitch, or you're a dead man," said the bearer of the rifle.

Fargo froze, aware that they were surrounded by men in brown uniforms. He wanted to pound his own head against one of the boulders for being so thoughtlessly careless. Then a strutting peacock walked around in front of him, and smirked.

"We meet again, mister, as I told you we would," Major Mortimer Gatz crowed. He motioned, and a militiaman stripped Fargo of the Henry and the Colt. Nodding at the dead wolves, he said, "I owe those creatures a debt. I had nearly decided to give up and head back in the morning when we heard the shots. They helped us pinpoint where you were."

Eight soldiers ringed them. Two others were a ways off, bringing up their mounts.

Gatz stepped over to Wagon Annie, who slumbered blissfully on. "Look at this. Even traitors to their own kind can seem like perfect angels when they're asleep." He nudged her leg with a boot. She failed to do more than stir and mumble, so he kicked her again, harder.

"Ow!" Annie yelped, snapping up. At the sight of her nemesis, she grabbed for the bullwhip, but Gatz gestured and two soldiers were on her before she could uncoil it. She flung lusty oaths at them, struggling mightily to no avail.

Gatz was a master of the arrogant sneer. "My, my. Such a mouth. You don't even pretend to be a lady, do you?"

"Go to hell, you miserable bastard," Annie spat. "I've seen how you look at me at times. You have a filthy mind, you—"

The major's hand slashed, the slap loud and crisp. "How dare you!" he thundered, going purple in the face. "How *dare* you!" Beside himself, he slapped her again, then again, the last one drawing blood at the corner of her mouth. Fargo started to rise, to go to her aid, and had a rifle muzzle shoved into his ribs.

Help came from an unlikely source. A militiaman wearing a sergeant's insignia grabbed the officer's arm as Gatz raised it to deliver another blow. "Enough, sir!"

Gatz was a hair's-width from going berserk. "Unhand me, Sergeant Preston! This is insubordination! I'll have you up on charges!"

Preston did not let go. He was a beefy man with a walrus mustache and sideburns that ran clear down to his bullish neck. "Think, sir. Think of what you're doing," he said in an even tone, as if soothing a temperamental child. "It's unbecoming of an officer." Pausing, he added meaningfully, "Look at the men, sir. They agree with me."

Fargo swiveled his neck. Almost to a man, including the pair who had him covered, their features betrayed blatant disgust. The major had blundered in the worst way.

Most men who lived on the frontier held women in high regard. For one thing, there were so few females that they were rated as precious as rare gems. No man who had never gone without seeing a woman for weeks or months at a stretch could possibly appreciate just how precious.

For another thing, the women who had ventured west were a hardy bunch who more than held their own. They worked as hard as any male, suffered the same whims of Nature and misfortunes of fickle fate. They plowed fields, helped uproot stumps, even took up arms to protect their families. In the process they earned the highest respect of men everywhere, so that, by and large, they were treated with the utmost courtesy.

Major Gatz harrumphed several times, then pretended his coat needed adjusting. Finally composed, he said, "Forgive me, gentlemen. My indignation got the better of me. It will never happen again."

Wagon Annie, her elbows held by the two troopers, managed to wipe her mouth with the back of a hand. "Maybe they'll forgive you, scum. But I never will. First chance I get, you're a dead man."

"Did you hear that, men?" Gatz capitalized. "A threat on my life. And you are all witnesses." He looked up as the horses arrived. "Perfect timing. Mount up, men. In three days we'll be back in Minneapolis, and Miss Standley and her friend will be placed in jail, where they belong."

Fargo was made to ride double with Annie. He was allowed to saddle the stallion himself after a militiaman tried and nearly lost a kneecap. The Ovaro did not like to be handled by strangers.

Mortimer Gatz noticed the empty peach cans, and kicked one. Rummaging through his saddlebags, he announced, "My shirts are missing. And what happened to my spyglass?" He turned and saw where Fargo had piled the sliced shirts after removing them from the pinto and the sorrel. "What the hell? So that's why we lost your trail."

"It's too bad you weren't wearing one when we cut them up," Annie said.

The officer ignored her. Going to the pinto, he found his telescope in Fargo's saddlebags, where Fargo had put it after Annie gave it to him. "Ah!" Gatz exclaimed. "I'll add theft to the charge of horse stealing and all the others."

Presently, the Minnesota Militia headed due east. Late in

the afternoon they came to the road between Minneapolis and Fort Ripley, and swung to the south.

Major Gatz was in a fine mood. He rode next to Fargo and Wagon Annie, prattling on about how one day he would be an important man in the territory, how his stint as a militia commander was the stepping stone to a higher ambition. "Mark my words. I will be governor eventually," he grandly predicted. "From there, who knows? The prospect of federal office is appealing. I can easily see myself running for President one day."

"You're a lunatic," Wagon Annie snorted.

"Am I?" Gatz clucked merrily. "It shows how little you know, my dear. Why, capturing you alone is enough to propel me into the governor's chair. It's a real feather in my cap."

Annie took the bait. "How so?"

"Think, woman, think. Most people despise the savages you think so highly of. When they hear that you've been funneling repeaters to the Santees, they'll be outraged. And profoundly grateful that I brought you in before you armed the entire tribe."

"How many times must I tell you that—" Wagon Annie tried to say.

"Please, don't insult my intelligence," Major Gatz said. "The case against you is ironclad."

"You don't have a lick of evidence, you jackass."

"Don't I?" Major Gatz said, and reached down to pat Fargo's Henry, which he had strapped to his own saddle. Fargo had thought it curious at the time. Now he understood, and it was all he could do to keep from smashing the conniving snake in the mouth. "Or is it mere coincidence that we found your partner in possession of the same kind of rifle you've sold to the heathens?"

"But Skye isn't my partner!" Annie said.

"So *you* say," Major Gatz said. "I daresay the good citizens of Minnesota will look at it differently."

Wagon Annie leaned toward him, her hand balled, but

Fargo stopped her from swinging. "How do you live with yourself, Gatz?" she railed. "How can you stand to look into a mirror, you snake?"

"Oh, please," Gatz said, and might have gone on gloating had he not realized that the soldiers in front of them had halted. He did, too, saying, "What the devil?"

Fargo glanced around. Ahead was a bend. To reach it, the patrol had to go past a rider who barred their path, a tall figure dressed in a black frock coat and broad-brimmed black hat, a man who favored a red sash and a pearl-handled nickel-plated Remington. It was the last person Fargo expected to see: Ethan Lee.

11

Instead of being glad to see a friendly face, Skye Fargo was suspicious. Ethan Lee had no reason to be there in the middle of nowhere. The gambler would not be welcome at Fort Ripley. Professional cardsharps were never permitted to do more than stay the night at remote posts, since the Army took a dim view of having its soldiers fleeced of their hard-earned wages.

Fargo recalled Wagon Annie's warning that the man in black was hiding something. Was he maybe in league with the gun traffickers? Fargo's instincts told him no, but he had misjudged a few people before.

Major Gatz moved to the head of the column. "Who are you, sir?" he demanded. "I have the feeling that I've seen you somewhere before, but I can't quite place you."

Lee, smiling, nudged the bay forward. His right hand held the reins close to his red sash, almost brushing his fancy pistol. "We've never been introduced," he said amiably. "But I know who you are, of course. Everyone in the territory has heard of Major Mortimer Gatz."

The peacock puffed up and beamed at his troops as if to say, "See how famous I am?" To the gambler he said, "I still believe we've met before. Recently, too."

Ethan Lee drew rein next to the officer, and nodded at Fargo and Wagon Annie. "They seem to be your prisoners."

"They are!" Major Gatz declared. "They've been selling rifles to the Sioux. We caught them dead to rights. It won't be long before they're the guests of honor at a necktie social."

It was a figure of speech, another way of saying they would be hung. Fargo frowned, studying the man in black. It was unrealistic to expect Lee to help. They were acquaintances, not the best of friends. The gambler had no cause to risk his hide on their behalf.

"You'd string up a woman?" Lee asked Gatz while switching the reins to his left hand. "My, you are a vicious bastard, aren't you?"

The major was quick to take offense. "I won't abide being talked to like that! Tell me who you are and what business you have in this area, or I'll take you back to Minneapolis for questioning. I think—" Gatz stopped and blinked several times. "Hold it! I remember now! You were with Fargo at the North Star Saloon! So you must be in cahoots with them! I'm placing you under arrest, too."

"I don't think so," Lee said casually, and suddenly the pearl-handled Remington was in his right hand.

It was one of the fastest draws Fargo had ever seen, fast enough to rival his own, and he had practiced for countless hours to become better than most any man alive.

Many gamblers were proficient with revolvers. They had to be, to protect themselves from drunks and rowdies and the accusations of poor losers. But Ethan Lee was exceptional.

A few of the militiamen grabbed for their rifles, freezing when the man in black extended his arm toward their commander and cocked the Remington. "No one try anything," Lee warned. "If you do, you'll be hauled before a federal judge on charges of attempted murder of a federal officer."

For a few moments, as the words sank in, no one so much as moved. Then Major Gatz barked, "A what? Do you take us for simpletons, sir? You're no more a federal officer than I am!"

Ethan Lee looped the reins around his saddle horn, and slipped his left hand under his frock coat. He produced a small envelope and handed it to the officer. "See for yourself, Major. You'll find my credentials in order."

Confusion and disbelief twisted Gatz's face as he opened the envelope and took out two sheets of paper. His eyes widened. "Why, it says here that you're a captain in the U.S. Army, that you're on special assignment. And this letter is signed by Simon Cameron, the Secretary of War!" He examined the other sheet, his astonishment growing. "This can't be! It's a letter from President Lincoln himself, granting you unlimited access to federal facilities and the right to command federal troops as you see fit."

"Satisfied now?" Ethan Lee said.

Fargo and Wagon Annie exchanged glances. Fargo was as amazed as the militiamen. If not for Annie's intuition, Lee would have hoodwinked him completely.

Major Gatz, true to form, was not satisfied. "So you're claiming to be some sort of secret federal agent? Is that it?" He wagged the letters. "How do I know these are authentic? How do I know you didn't forge them to bail yourself out of trouble?"

Now it was Ethan Lee's turn to be surprised. "Everyone told me that you're nearly as dumb as an ox, but I think they've got it backwards." He took his credentials and stuffed them into an inner pocket. "You will release Fargo and Miss Standley, Major. They are innocent."

To Fargo, it seemed as if the hothead popinjay was about to have a stroke. Gatz sputtered. He hissed. He speared a finger at them.

"Like hell I will! A jury will decide their guilt. As for you, sir, you will accompany us back to Minneapolis so I can confirm your claim."

Lee shook his head. "I don't have the time to spare. I'm after the gun traffickers, too, and I could use your help in hunting them down."

"You think I trust you?" Gatz rasped. "For all I know, this could be a ploy to lure me and my men into an ambush. We're not going anywhere with you."

Ethan Lee sighed. "Pathetic." Bending, he relieved the major of his side arm. "So you won't get any ideas," he said, then he addressed the rest of the patrol. "I'll only say this once. Any man who interferes will answer to the President. Sit right where you are until we're gone." Lee rode up next to the Ovaro. "You two are coming, aren't you?"

"Help you catch the real culprits?" Wagon Annie said, sliding off. "Need you ask?" She stepped to the major's mount and grinned wickedly. "Mind if I borrow your horse again? I'll try not to let the wolves eat this one." When Gatz did not reply or budge, she went to seize his leg.

"All right," the major said bitterly. "Have it your way. But this isn't over."

Fargo retrieved the Henry and rode to the end of the line, where two troopers rode double. One of them had his Colt and forked it over without being asked. He covered the soldiers as Lee and the redhead rode on past, Annie clutching her precious bullwhip.

Sergeant Preston watched intently. "Major Gatz, sir," he said. "What if that man is who he says he is? Isn't it our duty to help him?"

"Your duty is to do as I tell you," the officer responded. "Until we verify his claim, we are not lifting a finger on his behalf."

Preston disagreed. So did several others. An argument broke out as Fargo wheeled the pinto and overtook Annie and the captain. He did not take his eyes off the militiamen until a turn hid them.

Ethan Lee chuckled. "How *do* you manage to get into so much trouble, friend? If I were you, I'd give up living on the frontier. Go back East, and take up painting or knitting. You'll live longer that way."

Fargo was not amused. He had too many burning questions. For starters, "Why didn't you confide in me once you learned I was working for Colonel Williams?"

"My orders were to tell no one, including the colonel,"

Lee answered. "Besides, how did I know I could trust you? Or Miss Standley here?"

"Did you trail us from Minneapolis?"

"No. I was spying on the government's prime suspect, waiting for him to make a move. He caught me off guard by sneaking out of town in the middle of the night a couple of days after you left with Beckworth and Gatz. I've been shadowing him ever since."

"You know who is to blame?" Wagon Annie cut in.

"Let's just say that my superiors have a strong hunch," Lee said. "Secretary Cameron had the account books of the New Haven Repeating Arms Company examined to see who has purchased Henrys in large quantities. He suspected that it would be a Southern sympathizer."

"Why?" the redhead asked.

Lee glanced sharply at her. "Don't you read the newspapers, Miss Standley? Don't you know what is happening back East?" He paused. "Several Southern states have already seceded from the Union, and more are bound to do the same. President Lincoln will never stand for that, so war is bound to break out."

"Americans fighting Americans?" Annie said. "It will never happen."

"I wish that were true," Ethan Lee said sincerely. "The situation is a powder keg just waiting to explode. And then this business with the Santees came along."

"How does the South fit in?" Fargo probed.

"Secretary Cameron believed that someone with Southern ties was arming the Sioux to keep the federal government from transferring troops to the East, where they will be sorely needed when the war breaks out. As it turns out, he was wrong."

"All I want to know is the name of the guilty party," Wagon Annie said. "I can't wait to give him a taste of my lash for all the grief he's brought me."

"I'd rather surprise you," Lee said, and would not say more even though Annie pestered him for minutes on end.

It gave Fargo much food for thought. Like so many frontiersmen, he had not paid much attention to the brewing conflict between the North and South. Why should they, when it had scant effect on their personal lives? Relatively few people west of the Mississippi owned slaves, so it just wasn't much of an issue there yet.

In addition, the Eastern states were so distant that sometimes it seemed as if what went on back there might as well take place on another planet.

Fargo clucked to the stallion so it would keep up with the captain and the redhead. Maybe he had been wrong in not deciding where his own sympathies lie. If war did break out, what would he do? Whose side would he be on?

Lee faced him. "I know your reputation, Skye. I'm the first to admit that you're a better tracker than I am. So I'd be obliged if you would take over the chore."

The road had been churned up by the hoofs of the mounts belonging to the Minnesota Militia. Fargo scoured the torn turf, but saw no other sign to speak of.

"I was afraid of that," Lee said when informed. "Let's hope we don't lose them. I would hate to let the President down with so much at stake."

It was not until they had passed the point where the militia patrol had emerged from the forest and turned south that Fargo discovered recent tracks made by a large party heading north. He counted eleven packhorses and mules, plus nine men.

"That's more than I bargained on," Ethan Lee said. "The brains behind this outfit isn't taking any chances. He doesn't trust the Sioux one bit."

The pack train had gone on for another five miles. That was when a tenth man had ridden back from up ahead, and the whole party entered the trees on the right side of the road. Fargo guessed that the tenth rider had been a lookout, sent to forewarn the pack train should an Army patrol out of Fort Ripley come on down the road.

"They're heading east?" Ethan Lee said. "I heard that Red Wing's village is north of here, up near Leech Lake."

"Red Wing isn't involved," Wagon Annie said, and related her encounter with the chief as they trotted into the undergrowth.

Fargo concentrated on the tracks. One rider, perhaps the leader, had spent a lot of time riding up and down the line, most likely insuring that all went well. The train did not deviate from its new course once. The gun traffickers knew right where they were going.

Soon the rolling woodland was dotted by lakes of all sizes. The men guiding the pack animals made no attempt to conceal their trail. Having done this before and not been caught, they were overconfident.

"How close would you say we are?" Ethan Lee inquired.

"No more than an hour behind now," Fargo said. The mules and horses were so heavily loaded that they were limited to a brisk walk. If each carried three crates, and each crate contained a half-dozen repeaters, a conservative estimate, then the gun traffickers had close to two hundred rifles.

Two hundred! With that many, there would be no stopping Fire Thunder. The firebrand would blaze a path of blood and destruction from one end of the territory to the other.

"There's not much daylight left," the federal operative observed. "I'd like to catch up with them before the sun goes down."

"We will," Fargo promised.

A rosy crown framed the western horizon when he caught sight of riders and animals threading through firs in the distance. Pointing them out to his companions, he moved into cover until the pack train plodded out of sight.

Ethan Lee was overjoyed. "Now all we need to do is catch their leader in the act of transferring the Henrys, and we have them," he said.

"You aim to wait until the Santees arrive?" Fargo said

skeptically. "The three of us against fifteen or twenty guns?"

"It would be suicide," Lee agreed, and bestowed his charming smile on the redhead. "That's another reason I brought you along, Miss Standley. We're no more than a day's ride out of Fort Ripley. I'd like for you to ride there and lead Captain Beckworth back. Do you think you can?"

"Does a duck quack?" Annie rejoined.

"Here. You'll need this." From his saddle scabbard Lee pulled a Sharps. He also gave her an ammo pouch. "We're depending on you, ma'am."

The redhead winked at him. "Don't fret, fancy pants. I won't let you down. Just ask Skye. I always hold up my end." Laughing lustily, she spurred the militia mount westward and was soon lost in the shadows.

"Did I miss something there?" Ethan Lee asked.

Fargo reined to the northeast to parallel the pack train. Annie had agreed so readily that he suspected she had taken a shine to the dashing young officer.

Over the next hill glistened a sizable lake, the surface painted vivid red and orange by the setting sun. At the west end the shore was flat and grassy, ideal for a camp. The gun traffickers pitched a single large tent near the water, tethered their animals in two strings, one on either side of the site as living barriers against a surprise attack, and posted two men as guards at the open end of the square.

"Pretty shrewd," Lee remarked. "You'd think they had military training."

"Do they?" Fargo quizzed. He did not appreciate being left in the cold when he was risking his life on the captain's behalf.

"Not that I know of," Ethan Lee said. "They're just being cautious, and I can't blame them."

Dismounting at the top of the hill, they moved down to a bench that overlooked the encampment. Fargo saw a gunman tending the fire, men gathering wood, others taking care of the stock. Dozens of long crates were stacked near the tent. Inside it a lantern glowed, silhouetting someone who paced from front to back.

"He's as nervous as a caged cougar, and I don't blame him," Ethan Lee whispered.

"Who is it?"

"You'll see soon enough," Lee said.

The very next moment the tent flap parted, and out came a tall man dressed in an expensive set of clothes and an immaculate coat that Fargo had seen once before. He could not say he was in any way shocked. It had to be someone with a means of funneling a large amount of rifles across the country, someone just like Edward Wallace.

"Head of Wallace Freighting. You know him? His company was one of only a few that purchased a large consignment of Henrys. Wallace told the manufacturer that he planned to arm his drivers with them. Secretary Cameron grew suspicious when he learned that none of them had received one yet."

"But why?" Fargo said. "A man as rich as he is, what does he stand to gain?"

"It's not the money Wallace is interested in," Lee said. "As near as we can figure, it's the power. Annie isn't the only small freight operator he'd like to drive out of business."

Fargo was still at a loss. "How does inciting the Santees to go on the warpath help him? His wagons will have just as hard a time getting through as all the rest."

"True, every freighting firm will suffer," Ethan Lee concurred. "But Wallace will suffer the least. His outfit is the biggest. He has more capital, more funds in the bank. All he has to do is sit tight and watch his competitors go under one by one."

"Then he can step in once the Sioux are beaten and take up right where he left off," Fargo said.

"With no competitors left."

In a twisted sense, Wallace's logic was flawless. But it was a sad reflection on the human race, Fargo mused, that anyone would be willing to sacrifice so many lives, to say nothing of the welfare of the entire country, for the sake of sheer power.

"Look!" Ethan Lee whispered, pointing.

A lone rider had galloped from the trees north of the camp. It was a Santee warrior painted for war. He approached slowly, warily, showing that the Sioux trusted Wallace as much as he trusted them. At a yell, many of Wallace's men gathered around their boss and went with him to greet the new arrival. One of Wallace's crew, a grizzled customer in buckskins and an old beaver hat, exchanged sign language with the Santee. Presently, the warrior wheeled his painted mount and swiftly departed.

"It would be nice to know what that was all about," Lee commented.

Fargo had tried to read the hand signs, but the pair were too far away. "My guess would be that Fire Thunder sent a scout on ahead to make sure Wallace had arrived and count how many men he has with him. I wouldn't put it past him to try and steal the rifles if he thought he could get away with it."

Ethan Lee looked westward, where the sun had relinquished the heavens to the stars. "Do you reckon the Santees will show up tonight yet?"

"No. They'll wait until tomorrow" was Fargo's assessment. Neither side would risk close contact after dark.

"Good," Lee said. "That gives Miss Standley plenty of time to reach Fort Ripley. Knowing Beckworth, he won't waste a second getting here. With any luck, we'll catch the entire bunch red-handed."

Fargo was not so sure. It would take Annie a full twelve hours to reach the fort. Even if Beckworth departed immediately, the patrol needed another twelve hours to reach them. He couldn't see Wallace and Fire Thunder lingering by the lake that long.

"We might as well make ourselves comfortable," the captain proposed.

Their horses came first. Fargo stripped off his saddle and gave the stallion a rubdown, using a handful of grass. After secreting the saddle and saddlebags in a patch of weeds, he glided down to the bench and relieved Lee so the federal man could tend to the bay.

Munching on jerked venison and pemmican, Fargo envied Wallace's outfit, who dined on a buck shot by one of their own. The heady aroma of brewing coffee made his mouth water.

Ethan Lee had switched his white shirt for a gray one when he returned. He had also removed his spurs and shifted his pistol farther under his frock coat to hide the white pearl grips. The man was a thorough professional.

"Been at this a while, haven't you?" Fargo said.

"Longer than any sane man would. I was a lowly lieutenant in the Fifth Cavalry until a year ago. By accident, I stumbled on a group of men with ties to the South stealing weapons from a federal armory. My men and I stopped them. Somehow, word reached Secretary of War Cameron. Before I knew it, I was in his office being asked if I were willing to devote my whole being, as he put it, to preserve the Union." Lee looked around him. "And here I am."

"Any regrets?"

"Not really. I believe in our country. I believe in what President Lincoln is trying to do." Lee paused. "How about you, friend? You'd be good at this line of work. Want me to recommend you to the secretary?"

Fargo did not have to ponder his answer long. "I'm happy doing what I do. The Army has called on me in the past, and they know they can count on me if they need me again. That's enough."

Gruff laughter and loud voices rose from the Wallace camp until well past midnight. Blankets were spread out ringing the tent and the crates, and that was where the men slept, rotating guards every few hours. The night was uneventful. Before first light the gun traffickers were up, getting ready for the arrival of their guests.

Fargo managed to catch a few hours of sleep. When the sun's golden glow was spreading across the north woods, he was prodded awake by Ethan Lee. Sitting up, he shook himself, then raised a hand to run it through his hair. Movement south of the lake riveted him in place. He leaned forward, puzzled by why Fire Thunder had seen fit to come up on the camp from that direction rather than the north. Then he saw what the newcomers were wearing.

Uniforms. It was Major Mortimer Gatz and the Minnesota Militia patrol.

12

Captain Ethan Lee spotted the figures a split second after the Trailsman. "What the hell?" he blurted, forgetting himself and starting to rise. "How did that lunatic get here?"

Skye Fargo lunged, throwing his arms around Lee's legs before the man in black exposed them to the cutthroats below. "Stay down!" he said, yanking.

Lee did not resist. Stupefied, he declared, "Tell me this isn't happening! That I'm having a nightmare! Gatz will ruin everything!"

A sweep of the camp showed Fargo that none of Wallace's outfit had noticed the militiamen. "The major isn't a total jackass," he mentioned. "He hasn't left the cover of the tree line yet. We're the only ones who can see him, and only because we're higher up." Peering closer, Fargo distinguished a person with flame-red hair near the center of the militia line. "There's your answer to how Gatz found out," he said. "He caught Annie."

"Again?" Lee said.

Fargo could guess how. Gatz, eager to pay them back, had the militia tracker dog their tracks. The patrol must have reached the spot where the pack train had turned off the road, about the same time that Wagon Annie was on her way out of the woods. Gatz would never let her go unmolested. He'd bound and gagged her, and brought her along. Damn him all to hell.

"Oh, God! Not now!" Lee suddenly said.

Riding out of the forest to the north were Sioux. Fire

Thunder and twelve fellow warriors were spread out in a skirmish line, approaching the encampment as they might a walled fort. The fiery renegade rode at the center, slightly in the lead of the rest.

One of Wallace's men spotted them and shouted. Edward Wallace, with most of his men flanking him for protection, moved to the open end of the square to greet the Santees.

In smooth precision the entire line swung to the west, around the tethered pack string on the north side of the camp, until the renegades were strung out across the open space.

Wallace and the same grizzled frontiersman who had translated the evening before now walked up to Fire Thunder, and a flurry of sign language ensued.

"Twenty-two," Lee said thoughtfully, totaling the combined odds. "We can take them if Gatz will stay put and follow my orders once I get over there." He swiveled to the south. "All I have to do is stick to the woods and—"

Fargo had been watching the tree line south of the lake. "Ethan!" he said urgently as the riders in brown began to form into a long line of their own.

"What is that fool doing?" the federal agent wondered.

"I'd say he's preparing to charge," Fargo speculated. Gatz had drawn his sword and was slashing imaginary foes in preparation for the real thing. His men were checking their single-shot carbines, all except for Sergeant Preston, who was saying something to Wagon Annie.

"No!" Lee said, moving to the edge of the bench. "Doesn't he realize he doesn't stand a prayer? Half those Sioux already have Henrys, and Wallace's crew are well armed. The militiamen will be cut down before they get halfway."

Gatz did not think so. At a bellow from him, a bugler shattered the morning quiet with a raucous battle refrain that Fargo could not identify. In smart formation the militiamen paraded into the open. Wagon Annie's horse, he noticed, did not move. She was being left behind, all alone, defenseless.

Lee smacked a hand into his other palm. "Damn! And there's nothing we can do for them! Not a blessed thing, or we'll be killed ourselves."

"You're forgetting Annie," Fargo said, and was off up the slope in long lopes that brought him to the Ovaro in seconds. Frantically, he threw on the saddle blanket and the saddle. Fingers flying, he tightened the cinch, strapped on his saddlebags, and rose in the stirrups as a second martial refrain knifed the brisk morning air.

The new notes were different. Fargo went over the side in a rush, and saw that the militiamen had goaded their mounts into a rapid walk. Near the middle was Major Mortimer Gatz, his saber held as stiffly as his spine. This was probably the moment the bigot had waited for all his life, the glorious moment when he would garner the military victory he so desperately needed to launch his political career.

"Skye, wait!" Ethan Lee cried, but Fargo was not about to. Already he saw that Wagon Annie's mount was straying into the open. Pounding on past the captain, he headed for the bottom.

In the camp, all was bedlam. Wallace's men were scurrying every which way, Wallace roaring orders like a madman. The Sioux, by contrast, were as composed as if they were out for a Sunday jaunt in a big city. Clustering together, they turned to meet the militia advance.

Fargo heard Lee call his name one last time, but he did not look back. The federal agent was on his own. Rescuing Annie was more important than anything else. At the base of the hill, he veered to the right to loop around the militia. None of them had seen him as yet. To a man, the mostly young soldiers had eyes only for the renegades who were now moving out to meet them.

A glance back revealed that Ed Wallace was organizing

his cutthroats into a defensive line on the south side of the camp. Nearly all of them had rifles.

Once more the bugler cut loose. At the signal, Major Gatz cried a command, and the Minnesota Militia broke into a trot. It was stupid. It was magnificent. And the outcome was foreordained.

Fargo saw a Santee look in his direction, yip, and break away from the war party to give chase. Another joined in. Thankfully, the remainder were intent on the troopers. He lashed the reins, goading the stallion into a literal race for life.

The Minnesota Militia were holding formation nicely. Fargo was almost even with their strung-out row when Major Mortimer Gatz spied him. Incredibly, the officer grinned and saluted with the saber. Then Fargo was past the militiamen, slanting toward the tree line and the roan that was nibbling at grass in plain view.

The two warriors after him prudently swung wide of the militia also. One waved a lance overhead, the other was armed with a rifle. A new Henry, like Fargo's own.

For the last time the bugle sounded. Mortimer Gatz shrieked, and the Minnesota Militia spurred their animals into a gallop. They were almost to the Sioux now. At the major's shout, a sustained volley rang out. But they were firing on the fly, trying to hit targets with their mounts pitching and swaying under them. They smashed Santees to the grass, but too few. Far too few.

Fire Thunder and his renegades responded in kind. Only their volley did not taper off. Those who had Henrys fired and fired and fired, their leaden hail slamming into the hapless militiamen, hammering the soldiers from their saddles.

Half the Minnesotans were dead or dying, but that did not slow the rest. Major Gatz still in the lead, they rammed into the knot of Sioux, scattering warriors before them, dropping two or three more. Then, miraculously, they were through; they were bearing down on the encampment itself. But by this time only four were left.

Major Gatz did not seem to realize it. Or if he did, he didn't care. Elevating his saber, he bawled his last command. The remnants of the Minnesota Militia patrol were thirty feet from Edward Wallace, the man whose lust for power rivaled Gatz's own, when Wallace bellowed and the killers under him unleashed a withering fusillade.

To a man, the militiamen went down. Somehow, Gatz got to his feet. So did Sergeant Preston, who, though riddled, lurched to his superior's side. Shoulder to shoulder they stood, pistols clutched in bloody hands. Preston got off a single shot. Then a second fusillade tore the life from their crumpling bodies.

The Sioux and their cutthroat allies swarmed toward the sprawled forms to insure their foes were dead.

By this time Fargo was close enough to Wagon Annie to see her struggling against her bonds. Her wrists were tied behind her back, her legs to the saddle. If her horse should spook, she would be in grave danger. At the moment, she was twisting her mouth back and forth to work the gag loose. Her gaze went past him and widened.

The two Santees were not yet near enough for the warrior with the rifle to shoot, but they would be soon.

In a spray of dust, Fargo reined up. Vaulting to the ground, he dashed to the roan and snatched the dangling reins. A slash of the toothpick, and he freed Annie's wrists. Another slash, her legs could move. She tore the gag from her mouth herself, and hollered, "Let's skedaddle! They're almost on top of us!"

The boom of a rifle accented her point. Fargo was astride the stallion in a twinkling, jerking his Henry out. Lead buzzed past his ear as he fixed the front sight on the warrior holding the rifle, and cored the man's chest. That did not deter the Santee hefting the lance. Howling like a banshee, the Sioux charged fearlessly. Fargo did not give him a chance to fling his weapon.

The shots drew the interest of Fire Thunder. Yipping and

waving, he led the war party in an enraged rush around the end of the lake.

"Hell!" Annie exclaimed. "We're in for it now!"

"Stay close," Fargo advised, cutting into the pines as slugs clipped the branches around them. Low limbs tore at his clothes, at his face. He plunged through a thicket, weaved among woodland giants. Shaking the Sioux would not be easy. They knew the land; they knew every trick.

Turning due east, Fargo rode hugging the saddle. Annie followed his example, the roan doing a fine job of keeping up with the pinto. After traveling a hundred yards, he angled toward the tree line.

To their rear, the crash of brush and lusty cries were proof the Santees were searching. It would not take competent trackers like them long to figure out which direction Fargo had taken. He had to come up with something, and come up with it fast.

Another hundred yards were covered. The encampment was still in an uproar. From what Fargo could see, Wallace was having his men pack up and get ready to leave. The appearance of the militia had rattled the freighter. Fargo smiled. Unwittingly, Wallace had played right into his hands.

Yet another hundred yards, and Fargo left cover, crossing a grassy belt to the shore. They were now far enough from the camp that it was unlikely any of the gun traffickers would spot them. Fire Thunder and the other Santees were off in the trees. Fargo would never have a better opportunity.

Tall reeds choked the east end of the lake. Fargo had seen the growth earlier from up on the shelf. Now, urging the stallion into the water, he made for it. The water level rose to just under the pinto's belly.

"I hope to blazes you know what in the hell you're doing, handsome," Wagon Annie whispered. "If it were me, I'd light a shuck and not stop until I reached Maryland."

Some of the reeds were brown and crinkly, all had thin edges that doubled as razors. Fargo cut himself twice pushing stems aside as they penetrated into the middle. Here the reeds hemmed them in, the blades higher than their heads. "Keep your horse quiet," he warned, and covered the Ovaro's muzzle with his left hand.

"I don't like this, not one bit," Annie whispered. "We're sitting ducks if they figure out where we are."

"Trust me."

"Hmmph. No woman in her right mind ever trusts a man," she quipped.

The banter was for her sake, to ease the tension that had drained her face of color. Fargo stiffened as muffled voices jabbered in the Santee tongue. Quietly parting some of the reeds, he laid eyes on Fire Thunder and the war party clustered near the trees. They had stuck to the trail that far, but had not yet seen the tracks leading down to the lake.

"We're dead!" Annie reiterated.

Two of the warriors headed for the shore. Fargo brought up the Henry, but it was barely above his waist when Fire Thunder snapped toward Wallace's camp. The commotion had finally perked his interest. The warrior scowled, waved a Henry overhead, and raced westward. Where he went, the rest were always right behind.

"What in tarnation?" Wagon Annie marveled.

Fargo could have told her that they owed their lives to Wallace, that when Fire Thunder realized the freighter was trying to leave without handing over the repeaters, the renegade had forgotten all about them.

As soon as the Sioux were stick figures in the distance, Fargo moved eastward onto the shore and then northward into the vegetation. When he reined westward, Annie swore.

"Sometimes I worry about you, lover. I truly do." She came near enough to put her hand on his. "Where do you think you're going? In case it ain't sunk in yet, those varmints are out for our blood. We should be going *away* from them, not *toward* them."

"We have to stay close to the rifles," Fargo said. The Henrys were the key to preventing a massacre. Deprive the Sioux of them, and no lives would be lost. Or so he hoped.

"Since when is that our job? Captain Lee is still out there somewhere, I gather? Then, let him risk his hide if he wants. It's what he is paid to do. Me, I've been shot at enough these past few days to last me a lifetime."

"I thought you wanted to get even with Ed Wallace?"

The redhead went rigid. "Wallace? He's the brains behind this? The traitor who is selling the rifles?" Unconsciously, she fingered her shoulder where her bullwhip normally hung. "That puts everything in a whole new light. Count me in, big man."

The hubbub at the camp grew louder, more strident. Fargo hurried. A break in the trees afforded him a glimpse of Ed Wallace and Fire Thunder, in heated disagreement. The eight other Sioux were huddled near where the string of pack animals had been tethered south of the fire. Those animals were now being loaded by fully half of Wallace's crew, while others tended to taking down the tent or saddling mounts.

"You watch," Annie whispered. "Wallace will get away, clean as a whistle. Men like him never get caught. They're above the law."

"Man-made laws, maybe," Fargo said. But there were other laws, natural laws, higher laws. Never, ever renege on a deal with the Sioux was one of them. Or, as a deacon might put it, when people did business with the devil, they should take it for granted that they would be burned.

Fire Thunder's mood matched his name. Features ablaze, he came close to striking Wallace with his quirt when the freighter pushed past his horse, dismissing him as if he were one of Wallace's lackeys. Lightning dancing in his eyes, he rode toward the other warriors.

The frontiersman who had translated sign for Wallace

was just as upset. Nervously running a hand over his rifle, he backed up. Of all the whites, he was the only one who sensed that something was dreadfully wrong. Ironically, he was the first to die when the Santees vented fierce war whoops and opened fire.

The onslaught was swift. It was brutal. The Sioux were on the men loading the pack animals before the gun traffickers could lift a finger. Three died amid screeches and screams. The man dismantling the tent was the next to go down, his chest a sieve spouting scarlet geysers.

Wallace and the last few turned at bay. They battled savagely, but briefly. One of the Santees catapulted from his onrushing steed. Then all the whites were dead except for Edward Wallace, and he had bloody wounds on his right leg as well as his left shoulder.

Down on his knees, swaying as if drunk, Wallace attempted to pull a pistol from under his expensive coat. He blanched when Fire Thunder swung to his side, reached low, and tugged the revolver from his grasp. "Bastard!" Wallace cried in strangled defiance. "I knew I couldn't trust you!"

Fire Thunder examined the revolver, a Smith & Wesson, grunted, and tossed it to another warrior. From a beaded sheath, he drew a Green River knife, the type favored by mountain men and buffalo hunters for their keen edge. Ordinarily, Green River knives were used to skin hides. Fire Thunder gripped Wallace by the throat, bent the freighter backward, and put his blade to the same use.

At Wallace's initial shriek, Wagon Annie turned away and covered her ears. "You can't let them do that, Skye," she said. "It ain't right."

Fargo begged to differ. Edward Wallace had it coming. In fact, a learned university professor Fargo had once guided in search of rare plants, a man who knew all the great books and was always prattling on and on about the finest thinkers of the age, would have said it was "poetic justice."

Edward Wallace, the schemer who had plotted to insti-gate an Indian uprising resulting in hundreds dead, found himself one of the first victims of the Sioux he had tried to use as puppets. What could be more fitting?

Annie's roan shied at the next shriek, so piercing it shocked a flock of sparrows into flight and caused a num-ber of packhorses and mules to act up. "How can you stand it?" she said accusingly.

Fargo could abide it because he had seen worse, and be-cause he was not rash enough to rush out there and be shot to ribbons for the sake of a man who would have slain him with no more remorse than most people shed when they stomped on ants.

Fire Thunder took perverse delight in his work. When he was done, Edward Wallace lay quivering and whimpering, broken in body as well as spirit, the skin peeled from his chest and legs and rolled into tidy strips. Red rivulets trick-led from the holes where his eyes had been.

"Why have you stopped, you stinking heathen!" the freighter croaked. "If you have any decency at all, you'll put me out of my misery!"

The Sioux were busy finishing the job Wallace's crew had started. Nearly all the crates had been loaded. The pack horses and mules were being linked by rope into a single string. Every last weapon that belonged to the slain men was being collected, along with articles of clothing that struck the fancy of the victors.

"Please!" Wallace squalled, on the brink of hysterics. "For the love of God!"

Fargo raised the Henry. "Get ready to ride like a bat out of hell," he advised the redhead. But as his trigger finger tightened, a single shot rang out, from up on the hill to the west. Wallace's head whipped to one side, the temple blown outward in a gory spray of blood and bone.

"Who—" Wagon Annie said.

"Ethan Lee."

The Santees dived for cover. When no more gunfire rang

out, they poured lead at the hill, several leaping onto their warhorses to go find the rifleman. A shout from Fire Thunder brought them back. There was heated talk that ended with the Santees hustling the pack animals into the woods, the warriors spaced at ten-yard intervals.

Fargo had to hand it to their treacherous leader. Fire Thunder was being canny. Like him, the renegade knew that the rifles were what mattered, and Fire Thunder was whisking them away before more whites arrived. He motioned for Annie to keep low as the train passed within forty feet of their hiding place.

Bit by bit the crackle of twigs and the thud of hooves dwindled. Sparrows chirped again. Squirrels chattered. Fargo felt it was safe enough to venture into the bright sunlight.

From the other direction trotted Captain Ethan Lee. The special federal officer scanned the battlefield in disgust, indicating the body of Sergeant Preston. "What a waste of good men! Wallace's bunch had it coming, but those poor soldiers were just obeying orders."

Wagon Annie could not take her eyes off of what was left of Edward Wallace. "I wanted him to pay," she said softly to no one in particular, "but not like this. Never like this."

Fargo alighted. The Santees had torn the tent to shreds. Anything and everything they had branded as worthless had been busted and scattered wildly about. Dying horses had been left to expire. Some whinnied pitiably or feebly thrashed about. Off to the southeast a few mounts that had not been harmed were grazing. Any other time, the Sioux would have taken them. But the renegades had their hands full with the pack train.

Ethan Lee stayed on the bay. "There's only one thing to do. One of us must ride to Fort Ripley. The other has to follow the Santees and blaze sign. Which chore do you want?"

It would be safer going to the fort, but Fargo was more at

home in the woods, and they both knew it. "Fire Thunder is mine," he said, "I'll do what I can to slow him down."

Lee swiveled toward Annie, who had ridden off and was searching for something. "What about her? I vote she goes with me. Safer that way."

"It would be best," Fargo said. He could make better time alone. Since there was nothing of value worth saving, he lifted his foot to the stirrups.

Twenty yards away lay a dead Santee on top of a bow and quiver. In their haste to escape with the repeaters, the other Santees had neglected to collect their own dead.

It gave Fargo pause. He went over. The warrior had been hit in the forehead, then fallen backward. Fargo flipped the man to one side, tugged the quiver's sling over the Santee's shoulder, and helped himself to the smooth, finely crafted bow. He tested the sinew string by pulling it a few times.

"What can you hope to do with that relic?" Ethan Lee asked. "A bow against modern repeaters? You'd be riddled before you got off two shafts."

"Maybe" was all that Fargo would commit himself to. A plan was taking shape. An insane plan. But if it worked, he could stop the Santee uprising before any more lives were lost.

"Fellas!" Wagon Annie hollered cheerily. "Look at what I just found!" She swung her bullwhip in a graceful arc that ended with an explosive crack. "Now that I have Precious back, bring on those renegades!"

President Lincoln's special officer cleared his throat. "Actually, Miss Standley, I was thinking that you should go with me to Fort Ripley."

"You thought wrong, sugar. I'm not running off like a scalded dog. It's root hog or die, and I aim to stick with Skye."

"What would you do if I were to insist?"

Annie burst out laughing. "Why, I'd split that big black hat of yours down the center. And if you still insisted, I'd aim my whip a mite lower down."

Lee fidgeted, annoyed. "Why are females always so contrary?" He glanced at Fargo. "You know I'm right. She should leave. What would you do if you were me?"

"I'd keep in mind some advice an old-timer down in Santa Fe once gave me."

"Which was?"

"Never provoke a woman who can turn a bull into a steer with a flick of her wrist."

"You're making that up."

"Try her, then."

Ethan Lee was not foolish enough to do any such thing. Peeved, he reined the bay around, saying to Wagon Annie, "A smart poker player knows when to fold his hand. Stay with Skye if you want, Miss Standley, but you're making a mistake. You would be safer with me."

"Would I, now?" Annie responded, placing a hand at the small of her back and thrusting her bosom out, mimicking a habit dance hall girls had when they greeted new customers.

Fargo almost laughed when the President's special operative actually blushed.

"Soldier-boy," Annie went on, "the day I start to play it safe is the day I whittle my own coffin. Life is a gamble, day by day. We have to learn to accept the toss of the dice, or we might as well never get out of bed in the morning. And I've never been partial to quaking under the covers."

"You're a grown woman," Ethan Lee said irritably, not appeased. "You can do as you want." Raising his reins, he paused. "Just take care of yourself, you hear? I'm looking forward to treating you to a drink when we get back to Minneapolis." Something seemed to catch in his throat. "I would hate for anything to happen to you."

The reason why was as plain as the nose on Fargo's face. Annie saw it, too, and it was her turn to flush crimson. "Oh," she said. Then again, more softly. "Oh." A sly smile curled those rosy lips of hers. "You're on, Captain. Drinks for two, on you. I'll bet ten dollars right now that I can drink you under the table." She chuckled lustily. "Of course, if I do, I'll have to tote you to your room and tuck you into bed, won't I?"

"It's a deal," Ethan Lee said, and rode off beaming like someone had just given him a new lease on life.

Annie caught Fargo smirking at her, and blustered, "What are you looking at, mister? Can't a gal be friendly without someone thinking she's up to no good?"

Fargo was not about to answer. It would be the same as looking down the barrel of a cocked gun. Forking leather, he rode northward. The interlude had served to brighten Annie's mood and take all their minds off the horrors of the morning, but now they had unfinished business to attend to.

The pack train had left a trail a greenhorn could follow. It led due north, leaving Fargo no doubt that the renegades were heading for the vicinity of Leech Lake. He made no special effort to overtake them right away.

The Santees had a long, hard trek ahead of them. Unaccustomed as they were to handling pack mules, it promised to test their patience and their stamina. By the middle of the afternoon, Fargo calculated, the warriors would be tired and sore. That would make them prone to be careless. Which was exactly what he wanted.

Wagon Annie did not bend his ear. She knew enough to keep her eyes skinned and her mouth shut. Fargo lent her the Henry in case Fire Thunder sent warriors to scout the back trail. None appeared, though, and along about one o'clock the tail end of the pack train came into sight.

"Now what?" Annie said. "There are eight of them and only two of us."

Fargo bore to the left, into the pines, and applied his spurs. It was not long before they were close enough to hear the snort of plodding mules and horses, the rasp of rope on crates. Cautiously advancing, he saw that one of the warriors rode at the end of the pack train to goad stragglers.

Drawing rein, Fargo slid off and gave them to the redhead. "Stay here until the Sioux are half a mile ahead of you, then follow slowly."

"Where will you be?" Wagon Annie asked.

"I'll give a yell when it's safe for you to bring our horses," Fargo said, and turned to go. He had to hurry if he was to keep up with the train on foot.

"Wait a minute. That was no answer," Annie said. "If you're fixing to tangle with those varmints, then count me in."

Fargo had hoped that for once she would not kick up a fuss. "I'm going on alone."

"Oh, really? And what makes you think I'll listen to you any better than I did to that cute Captain Lee?"

In response, Fargo simply locked his eyes on hers.

The redhead recoiled as if slapped. She angrily opened her mouth to argue, then hesitated, the anger fading as fast as it had appeared. "You could scare babies to death with a look like that. All right. You've made your point. My stomach still hurts from Fort Snelling. I'll do what you want."

Adjusting the sling to the quiver, Fargo jogged northward. The Santees were not very watchful. He drew abreast of the middle of the pack train, where a pair of stubborn mules had balked and refused to go on. Four warriors were trying to prod them along. Among the four, Fargo recognized Runs Against and Makes Room. Both had been with Fire Thunder when the renegade confronted Red Wing. Runs Against, he recollected, had been the one who convinced Fire Thunder not to harm Wagon Annie.

Presently, Fire Thunder came galloping down the line. On discovering the cause of the delay, he leaped to the ground, picked up a heavy stick, and stormed toward the hind end of one of the irksome mules. Evidently, no one had ever told him that doing so was unhealthy. No sooner had he raised the stick than the mule lashed backward, one of its hooves catching him in the thigh.

The firebrand snarled and raised his rifle. He would have shot the mule dead had Runs Against and two others not talked him out of it. Fuming, he mounted his paint and made for the head of the line, barking at them over his shoulder.

Retracing his steps, Fargo moved stealthily toward the rear. The lone warrior there was impatiently waiting for the pack train to get moving again. He kept rising on his warhorse in an effort to see what was holding things up. In his right hand was a Henry.

Behind a wide trunk, Fargo stopped. He selected an arrow and notched it to the string. Extending the bow, he slowly drew the string back until his hand brushed his chin. Then, sighting down the shaft, he stepped into the open, fixed the barbed tip on the warrior's chest, and called out in the Teton Sioux tongue, "Drop the rifle!"

Whether the Santee understood or not was irrelevant. The warrior made no attempt to discard the Henry. Instead, he whipped the stock to his shoulder and took aim.

The arrow streaked through the air, almost too swiftly for the human eye to follow. Its tip sheared into the renegade below the ribs, wrenching him halfway around, exposing the point, which jutted from his lower back. Crying out, the warrior toppled.

Fargo was in motion before the body hit the ground. Whirling, he ran northward, sticking to the thickest cover. Runs Against and the other Sioux trying to spur the mules along had heard the shout, and were racing back along the trail. They flew on by in a flurry of dirt and dust.

Coming to a tree with a low limb, Fargo slung the bow over a shoulder, jumped up to grip the branch, and levered himself upward. Working higher to a fork shielded on all sides by heavy foliage, he cupped his hands to his mouth, directed his voice at the ground, and bellowed in the tongue of the Tetons, "Leave the rifles and go."

Shouts erupted. Fargo stayed where he was, his right hand on the Colt. Soon the crash of undergrowth showed that the war party was searching for him. Fire Thunder railed in fury, snapping at his fellows as if they were to blame.

Once a warrior passed almost directly under the tree, so close that Fargo saw the man's back. But that was the closest any of the Santees came. Within fifteen minutes, they had given up and returned to the pack train.

Fargo slid to a gap in the foliage. Normally, the Sioux would have scoured the forest until they found him. But Fire Thunder did not want to leave the repeaters unattended for very long.

The temperamental mules decided to cooperate this time. As the pack train wound northward, Fargo saw the dead warrior draped over his mount, which had been linked to the last animal in the train.

Every Santee had his rifle or bow handy. They constantly scoured the forest, on edge, as tense as coiled panthers. When a doe made the mistake of darting into the open, one of the Sioux nearly put an arrow into her.

Fargo stalked them, a shadow among the shadows. The dense growth enabled him to slip soundlessly along, with the Sioux none the wiser. Since the pack animals had to be held to a walk, Fargo soon caught up to the head of the string where Fire Thunder and two others rode.

Feral rage loomed on the renegade leader's brow. Fire Thunder did not like it when things did not go exactly as he wanted. He behaved like a five-year-old who had never grown up, and Fargo planned to use that to his advantage.

Passing the trio, Fargo ran until he came to an open spot the pack train must pass through if it continued on its current course. Leaning against an oak, he nocked another arrow to the bow. He did not have long to wait before the foremost Santees were so close that he could have beaned one with a rock.

Fire Thunder and one of the warriors were discussing something or other, while the third renegade was staring at a hawk soaring high in the sky.

Fargo drew back the string, took a breath, and stepped from behind the tree.

The warrior watching the hawk caught the movement out of the corner of an eye, and spun. His Henry jumped up, but his finger had not yet touched the trigger when Fargo's arrow sheared into his torso. The impact hurled him off his horse, into Fire Thunder.

A harsh bawl of fury rang in Fargo's ears as he spun and sped into a knot of pines. Flattening, he entwined himself around the base of a bole and hurriedly sprinkled fallen dead pine needles over his legs and back. He was none too soon.

Fire Thunder and the other Santees pounded to a halt twenty feet away. Their shouts drew the others. The six spread out, two of them skirting the pines. Both peered into them but did not spot Fargo.

Minutes of frenzied searching ended with a palaver. Fargo could see them but not hear them. Judging by their sharp gestures and angry expressions, it was obvious that half of the remaining Santees were for getting out of there before any more lost their lives.

Fire Thunder refused. He went on at length, then motioned for the band to return to the pack train. When one man balked, he grew incensed and would have struck the offender if not for Runs Against, who came between them. Reluctantly, the others did as their leader wanted.

Fargo stayed put. He watched as the pack animals started forward. Cupping his hands again, he resorted to the Teton language. "Forget the rifles and leave while you can."

The shout brought Fire Thunder and two others back. They prowled the area, one warrior poking a lance into every shadow and under every bush. Just when the warrior was about to enter the stand screening Fargo, Fire Thunder hollered and the three galloped to catch up with the pack train.

Disentangling himself from the trunk, Fargo rose and

brushed pine needles from his buckskins. He let a minute go by before jogging northward.

The Santees were more watchful than ever. Fargo loped around the warrior at the rear. Runs Against, Makes Room, and one other man were strung out at the middle. Fargo moved toward them on cat's feet. Twenty-five yards out, he sighted down a shaft at a crate on one of the mules that had given the Sioux such a hard time.

The arrow flew true. The mule promptly did what mules always did when scared half out of their wits. It bucked and brayed, nearly spilling its load, causing the nearest animals to break into a panic of their own. The warriors were hard-pressed to bring the string under control, but at last they succeeded.

Makes Room found the arrow embedded in the crate. Another dispute broke out. This time, Fire Thunder did not prevail.

Runs Against was the first man to ride close to the trees, hold his Henry in plain sight, then drop it in the grass. One by one, those who had Henrys did likewise. In a knot they galloped northward and did not look back.

A single warrior was left. Fire Thunder slid off his mount and turned toward the woods. Throwing back his head, he yipped long and loud, voicing his war cry, his challenge. He glared at the vegetation, his trigger finger lightly stroking the Henry's trigger.

Fargo lowered the bow and was about to let go when he changed his mind. It would be more fitting the traditional way. Sliding another shaft from the quiver, he moved forward, keeping a pair of pines between him and the renegade.

Fire Thunder shouted words Fargo did not need to understand to divine their meaning. The Santee was taunting him, daring him to show himself.

Fargo obliged. With the bow fully bent, he stepped to the left. Fire Thunder saw him. For perhaps five seconds, neither of them so much as twitched a muscle.

The renegade broke the spell by sweeping the Henry up and out, and firing smoothly, but as he did, the glittering shaft thudded into his chest, driving him back against his own horse. Dazed, he tried to steady the repeater. A second arrow whizzed into him within an inch of the first. Fire Thunder looked down at himself. A snarl ripped from his throat, and with his lips drawn back from his teeth, he pitched onto his face.

Colt in hand, Fargo strode out of the forest. At that juncture two horses drummed around the bend to the south. He pivoted, saw that it was Wagon Annie, and relaxed. "I thought I told you to stay put."

"Did you honestly expect me to listen?" The redhead stared at Fire Thunder. "You've done it, handsome! You've nipped the uprising in the bud!"

The Trailsman soberly regarded the wilderness north of them. For the moment, he had. But hatred still simmered on both sides. In time that hate would spill over, and Minnesota would run red with blood. "Let's take this pack train back to the lake and wait for the Army," he said.

"Fine by me." Wagon Annie chuckled. "But they won't get here until tomorrow. That means we'll be all by ourselves tonight." She leaned toward him, her lips forming a delicious oval. "What should we do to pass the time?"

"I can think of something," Skye Fargo said with a straight face.

*1860, the Wyoming territory
north of Red Canyon, where death
rides a mission of mercy . . .*

"Damn!"

Skye Fargo spit the word out as he ducked and felt the razor nick his cheek. Crouched, the razor still in his hand, the sound of the shot rang in his ears. The shot had come from a distance, a stray rifle bullet, much of the power gone from it as it thudded into the tree six inches from him. But it still had enough force to knock the little mirror out of the crook in the branch where he had set it.

"Jesus, can't a man get a morning shave around here," he muttered as he peered across the stretch of open land. More shots erupted, and then the wagon came into sight, canvas-topped, a driver whipping the team to go as fast as they could. Fargo saw the three riders appear, pursuing the wagon. Then he saw five more following. The riders were quickly catching up to their quarry, all of them bent on sending a steady stream of rifle bullets at the fleeing wagon.

Fargo stayed crouched at the edge of the forest of hackberry, where he had bedded down for the night, and watched the wagon driver swerve to try and avoid bullets.

As he watched, he saw a figure topple from the rear of the wagon. Two of the pursuers immediately poured bullets into it as they raced past. He frowned as he glimpsed two women inside the wagon when the canvas blew open at one side. The attackers were closing in on the wagon, and Fargo put down the razor still in his hand. Wearing only trousers, he reached out to where his gun belt hung on a branch, strapped it on as another figure fell from the careening wagon. Fargo rose and ran to where the Ovaro grazed nearby. There was no time to saddle up, he realized, and he pulled himself onto the magnificent black-and-white horse and went into an instant gallop.

Charging across the open land, he leaned forward in the saddle as he drew the big Colt, aimed, fired, and saw the rider alongside the wagon topple from his horse. The riders immediately slowed as they peered across at him. Fargo fired again, and saw another of the men fall sideways from his horse. But the other pursuers had come up, and Fargo ducked low as he saw the fusillade of bullets fired at him. He sent the pinto into a tight turn, streaked back to the stand of hackberry as bullets whistled past him, reached the forest, and plunged into the trees. He halted after he'd gone a dozen or so yards, and leaped from the horse's back to land in a six-foot high, thick cluster of sweet fennel. Sinking down at once in the blue-green leaves of the weeds, he peered through the fine filaments and saw four horsemen reach the edge of the forest, pause, and split up into two groups of two each.

Two moved to his right, two to his left. They had seen where he had raced into the forest and planned to close in on him from both sides. He uttered a silent, grim oath. They moved carefully, he noted and he glimpsed two more horsemen come to a halt just outside the treeline, stay back and wait. Fargo's eyes narrowed. He knew he could easily take down at least one with his first shot but that shot would tell them where he was and they'd pour a hail of bullets into the fennel. The four men were walking their horses, bending low in the saddle, listening as they scanned the thick forest undergrowth. Fargo knew he couldn't just lay low. The four horsemen were working their way back and forth. They'd come onto him in minutes and his lips drew back as his mind raced. He had to strike first without drawing the instant burst of return fire. He needed a few precious seconds, enough to make them run, not shoot.

Glancing at the big hackberry behind him, he half rose, holstered the Colt, and closed his hands around the lowest branch. Using all the power in his muscled arms and shoulders, he slowly lifted himself onto the branch, taking care not to disturb a leaf. He climbed onto the branch above and slid his long body around to the back of the tree trunk. His eyes went down to where the four horsemen were moving slowly toward each other, guns in hand. They were nearing the cluster of sweet fennel as Fargo drew the Colt and took aim. He counted off another few seconds and fired, one shot, first. The figure below and to his right seemed to jump in place in the saddle as the bullet thudded down through him, finally toppling from his horse. The others raised their guns, backed their horses, frowned as they searched for the spot to return fire.

Their confusion took only seconds, but they were the precious seconds of consternation Fargo needed. His next two shots sent two more of the attackers falling from their horses. The fourth man bent low in the saddle as he sent his horse racing from the forest. Fargo stayed in place and peered through the trees. The man joined the other two and all three decided to leave, turning their horses and galloping across the open land. Fargo stayed in place until they were out of sight before he swung down out of the tree and stepped to where the three lifeless forms lay silent and still. He went through each man's pockets, found coins, some paper money, keys, tobacco, but nothing that identified anyone. Lips pursed, Fargo called the Ovaro, swung onto the horse, and again rode bareback out of the forest.

He passed the spot where he had been shaving, his clothes and saddle still on the ground as he rode past. Out on the open land, he picked up the wagon tracks where the driver had fled west, followed the wheel marks around a curved line of serviceberry, and finally saw the wagon halted beside an arch of volcanic rock. The driver saw his approach and lowered the rifle he held in his hands. "The horses gave out," the man said as Fargo rode to a halt, a square face with a neatly cropped gray beard and bright blue eyes surrounded by a visage of crinkles and lines. "Where are they?" the driver asked.

"Gone," Fargo said, and saw the two women push their heads out of the wagon, both of their middle-aged faces drawn tight.

"We'd all be dead if you hadn't come along, mister," the driver said.

"Name's Fargo—Skye Fargo," the Trailsman said.

"Ben Smith," the man said, and Fargo guessed he had some seventy years on him.

"Why were they after you?" Fargo asked.

"Dammed if I know," Ben Smith said, and looked at the two women. The taller of the two spoke up, her eyes still holding disbelief and shock.

"No reason for it, no reason at all. We didn't know them. They just came at us and started shooting. I'm Grace Tumbley, and this is my friend Joan Ladden. My husband, Sam, and I organized the trip. They killed him with their first shot. He was riding alongside the wagon. We hired Ben on as driver."

"I'm guessing they were a passel of stinking dry gulchers looking to rob us," Ben Smith said.

"Most wagons don't carry enough money to be good targets for robbing," Fargo said.

"That's right, but some do," Ben said, and Fargo conceded the point with a half shrug.

"You tell people where you were going?" he asked Grace Tumbley.

"Of course. That's just natural when you're equipping a wagon," she said.

"Where were you headed?" Fargo questioned.

"Northwest, to find our way past the Caribou Range and keep going. We met in Green Springs and planned everything together."

"Green Springs? That's where I'm headed," Fargo said. "But one wagon going into the northwest country? That wasn't too smart an idea."

"Told them that," Ben Smith put in.

"There were four of us, plus Ben and two men who paid to come along," Grace Tumbley said. "We all decided that a single wagon wouldn't draw much attention from anyone, including Indians."

"Guess you decided wrong," Fargo said, and let his eyes go to the wagon, saw that it was a Texas wagon outfitted with top bows for a canvas roof and sides. Not as rugged as a Conestoga, it was nonetheless a fairly durable wagon—though the country they had headed for would give any wagon a terrible test. "Think your horses are ready to move?" he asked, and the man nodded. "Turn around, go back to Green Springs. I'll get my things and come help you with what has to be done," Fargo said.

Ben Smith nodded grimly, and Fargo put the Ovaro into a fast canter and rode back across the open land to the hackberry forest. He dismounted, and took a few minutes to put his pocket mirror back in place and finish shaving before he put the saddle on the horse. Setting out again, he found Ben Smith and the wagon halted. He dismounted to help tie the slain figures onto the backs of their horses. When the grim business was finished, he rode beside the wagon and heard the two women crying softly inside. "This is sure to be all over town a few minutes after we get there," Ben Smith said.

"Why?" Fargo asked.

"Green Springs has always been a kind of a starting place for wagon trains going north, west, even south. They take pride in being a good-luck place to start from. There's never been an attack like this," Ben said.

"Another thing that makes me wonder about it being a plain old robbery," Fargo said.

"You've another reason you're thinking about?" the old driver said.

"No, unfortunately," Fargo admitted.

"What brings you to Green Springs, Fargo?" Ben asked.

"Somebody asked me to meet them there," Fargo said.

"You're the one they call the Trailsman," the old driver said, and Fargo shot him a glance of surprise. "Put it together soon as I had a moment's breather." Ben laughed. "Your name and that Ovaro. You've a reputation, Fargo. I've driven for enough people to have heard it. You going to break trail for somebody?"

"Truth is, I'm not sure, but it's likely," Fargo said as the buildings of the town came into view. Green Springs turned out to be larger than he'd expected, Main Street wider, more buildings, more people, more bustle, more wagons. Most of them, he noted, were either Conestogas or smaller, light one-horse farm wagons. Ben Smith drew to a halt in front of a building with green-shaded windows and no name. "Undertaker's office?" Fargo asked, and he nodded.

"Thanks again for keeping a few of us alive," the old driver said.

"What'll the women do?" Fargo asked.

"Go back where they came from, I expect."

"And you?"

"People are always asking me to drive for them. I've a reputation of my own," he said with a touch of pride.

"Bet you do. Good luck, old-timer," Fargo said, and moved the Ovaro on. He'd reached the center of town when he drew up before the small building with the sign "SHERIFF" on the window. Dismounting, he went inside where two men looked up from a single desk, one wearing a sheriff's badge on a body with thirty pounds too much on it. "Bill Delbard?" Fargo asked, and the man nodded. "Skye Fargo," the Trailsman said, saw the man's eyes widen as he rose.

"Sit down, please. We've been waiting for you," the sheriff said. "We weren't sure if you'd reached Hank's place?"

"I did, and he told me you were waiting," Fargo said.

"Get Caroline," the sheriff said to the other man who quickly strode from the office. "It's Caroline Sanders who wants to see you. She got in touch with me, and I'd heard you were bringing a big herd in to Hank Bowers, so I got a message to him."

"I almost didn't make it," Fargo said, and told the sheriff about the attack on the wagon.

"Good God," the sheriff said when Fargo finished. "That's a new one out here."

"So Ben Smith said."

"Glad he came through. He's been driving trains out of here for years, mostly going into the southwest, though. He's a good old codger," the sheriff said as the door opened and a young woman strode into the office. She was tall and slender, with a small waist inside a dark blue jacket that allowed only the slightest swell of breasts.

"Thank heavens, you're here," she said to Fargo. "I'm Caroline Sanders. I asked the sheriff to find you for me." She extended a hand, and he felt a firm handshake. His eyes took in light yellow hair worn short, the color of bleached hay. At first glance her face was delicate, with pale skin, light blue eyes, and pale pink lips, but with strong features: a straight nose, firm jaw, and strong cheekbones. A longer glance showed that the pale blue eyes almost hid a cool, contained assurance. Caroline Sanders was an uncommonly attractive set of mixtures, he decided. She sat down across from him, and he glimpsed a long, slender calf.

"Hank Bowers said you sounded desperate," Fargo remarked.

"I am," Caroline Sanders said, leaning forward in her chair. "I need you for a mission of mercy. There's a wagon train of people with young children included who might be in danger of dying a terrible death. I've been working for Doc Dodson here in Green Springs for two years. Recently, he was hired to go on this wagon train because two of the women were close to giving birth."

"He left Green Springs on its own to do this?" Fargo frowned.

"They offered a good deal of money he said would buy a lot of medicine for use in town. That's the kind of man Doctor Dodson is. Besides, he wasn't going the whole way with the wagons, just long enough for the women to give birth. Then he planned to ride back at once on his own," Caroline said. "He felt I could handle things until then."

"Are you a nurse?" Fargo questioned.

"Not yet. I've been training under Doctor Dodson," Caroline said, reached into her pocket, and handed Fargo a letter. "This is why you're here. It came from Doc Dodson a few weeks ago." She sat back and waited as he began to read the straight, strong handwriting.

Dear Caroline,

I am dispatching this by a special messenger. I have become increasingly disturbed by certain things I've observed. I fear there may be smallpox on the train. You, of course, know what this means if it is so. The only one I've mentioned it to is Frank Turner, as he heads the train. As I am not sure, we decided it would be wrong to alarm the entire train, and perhaps cause unnecessary panic and conflict. But if I am right, you know how deadly this plague can be.

In the office cabinet there is enough serum to vaccinate everyone on the train. But time is everything. They must be vaccinated before there is an outbreak. You must get the serum to me before that happens and it is too late. You know how quickly this terrible plague can erupt.

Here is our route so far. We have traveled west. I wish I had taken the time to note landmarks. I can only recall a tall rock formation of arches and windows, a long forest of Gambel oak, and a huge field of columbine, plus innumerable rivers and valleys and mountains. It is Frank Turner's plan to cross the Green River, follow the west shore, and then turn west again to try and find Bear Lake. Then he plans to skirt the Wasatch Range into Idaho, go northwest to the Snake River Plateau, and perhaps hook up with the Oregon Trail there.

But so far we have only gone a small way, and I hope you can catch up to me soon. I pray to God I am wrong in my fears, but I dare not take that chance. Please hurry, my dear Caroline.

Doctor Dodson

Caroline spoke the moment Fargo lowered the letter. "I knew I'd never be able to pick up their trail, so I asked the sheriff for help. He told me that you were the very best and that you were expected at Hank Bowers. I've been biting my nails down waiting. I need your help. All those people need your help. You'll be paid for an act of mercy."

"The serum is in bottles?" Fargo questioned.

"Inside boxes," Caroline answered. "I've a wagon I bought at Schneider's wagon shop to carry them." Fargo's lips pursed as he looked down at the letter again. "What is it?" Caroline asked.

"This is a damn fool way to take a wagon train," he said. "I wouldn't be sure they can make it, plague or no plague."

"Why not?"

"I'll give you four quick reasons: the Shoshoni, Ute, Arapaho and Kiowa. They all prowl that territory," Fargo said.

"I understand there are some small communities and way stations along the way," she said.

"Small communities have a way of being massacred and way stations a way of being burned down," he sniffed.

"You saying we can't find the train?" she asked.

He ignored the assumption in the word *we*. "I'm saying it's damn unlikely. It's a trail almost a month old now, maybe covered over by rain, wind, and new grass. Then, one wagon traveling alone is easy pickings."

"I've hired six men to go along for protection," she said.

"Six?" he snorted. "Twenty might mean something."

"I couldn't afford twenty," Caroline snapped back. "I'm sure you've ridden trails through dangerous country before," she said with a touch of asperity.

"I try to keep the odds down," he said.

"How?"

"By not following fools," he said, and saw her lips tighten. The sheriff rose and started from the office.

"I'll leave you two to work this out," he said, and hurried outside. Fargo saw Caroline's eyes were on him with a penetrating coolness.

"It's really quite simple. I have to reach those wagons, and you have to help me," she said, more command than plea in her tone, and he noted the upward tilt of her chin.

"You've got something a little wrong there, honey," he said very quietly. "I'll help you but because I want to, not because I have to."

She waited a moment. "Yes, of course," she said, concession without retreat. The pale delicacy of her definitely had another dimension, he decided. "Then, we have an agreement?" she said.

"Yes," he said. She took a roll of bills from her jacket pocket and handed them to him.

"In advance," she said, and he nodded. "The wagon's waiting for me. I just have to pick it up, load it, and get in touch with Burt Hobbs. He's one of the men I hired. I'll be ready to roll by ten in the morning. We'll meet at Doc Dodson's building, the small white one up the street. I have living quarters there." She rose, a graceful, fluid movement, and he went outside with her, where night had blanketed the town. "Where will you stay tonight?" she asked.

"Maybe in town. Any place to stay here?" he said.

Her pale blue eyes surveyed him for a long moment. "Go to the Rest Inn, east end of town. You'll get a good sleep there." She paused again for a moment. "I know you'll find those wagons. You see, I've more confidence in you than you do," she said.

"Thanks," he said laconically. Being confident was one thing. Being naive was another, he commented silently and watched her hurry away, slender tallness held very straight. Prim, he thought, then changed it to aloof. He pulled himself onto the Ovaro and slowly walked the horse down Main Street, finally halted before an old, two-story frame house with filigreed woodwork on the outside and a small sign over the door. He dismounted and went inside, saw a large sitting room with a small front desk to one side. Four old ladies in the room looked up at him, all seated on worn sofas. Two stooped men, both with canes, moved gingerly across the floor. Two wizened old ladies were huddled under shawls over a checkerboard. A slow-moving little man who Fargo guessed weighed some ninety pounds, rose from behind the front desk.

"Want a room, young feller?" he asked.

"Maybe later, thanks," Fargo said. "Be back if I do."

"Not after ten. We don't take àny guests after ten," the man said.

"Got it," Fargo said as he returned to the Ovaro. He swung onto the horse again, decided his bedroll under a tree would be much preferable. It wasn't that the Rest Inn's guests were octogenarian, they were museum pieces, the place itself tomb-like, fit only for a good sleep, he thought, recalling Caroline's words. Riding back along Main Street, he slowed when he reached an oblong square of yellow light coming from a noisy building. He didn't need the sign to tell him it was the town saloon, but he frowned at the sign next to it that read: BED AND BOARD.

He tethered the Ovaro and went inside to find a typical saloon, sawdust-covered floor, and long bar, already half full of customers. A large-busted woman in a black gown greeted him with a smile that just managed not to be mechanical. "Room for the night?" Fargo asked.

"It's done," she said. "Give me your name, big man."

"Skye Fargo," he said, and she wrote in a small ledger on a table behind her, handed him a large key.

"Two dollars," she said. "I'm Clora. Just a room?"

"A bourbon and something to eat," Fargo said.

"Beef stew is real good tonight. Find yourself a table. I'll have Dolly serve you. She's not a girl I let wait on the average customer, but you don't look like there's anything average about you," the woman said.

He let his eyes stay on her, decided she wasn't giving him a stock line. "Thanks," he said, and made his way to a small table in a corner of the room. He relaxed with a sigh, glad he'd chosen not to stay at the Rest Inn. It had been a long, hard haul to Hank Bowers, and he didn't fancy spending the night in a museum. Caroline Sanders obviously had no idea what a tired, thirsty man needed to relax. A young woman appeared with his bourbon, and he took in a surprisingly fresh, open face without the hardness of most saloon girls. Her low-cut, black waitress outfit showed a full, high pair of breasts that pushed up over the top of the neckline.

"Bourbon's on the house. Our way of welcoming a new customer," she said. "I'm Dolly."

"You don't care that I won't be around long?" Fargo smiled.

"You might come back, they figure," Dolly said.

"How do you figure?" he asked, and Dolly's brown eyes took in his muscled physique. "Hope you do," she said. "We don't get many real good-looking men in here." She waltzed off, not waiting for him to answer. He ordered a second bourbon when she returned with his meal, and he enjoyed the open-faced freshness of her. She showed none of the jaded artifices of most saloon girls. He ate slowly, the stew tasty, and watched Dolly as she returned to lean both palms on the table. "We've satisfied part of you," she said. "Let me know if there's anything more you'd like satisfied." Again, no leer in her voice at all, no artificial suggestiveness, just an appealing honesty. His thoughts flicked to the trip that lay ahead, a mission of mercy that could well be a mission to disaster.

He took the key from his pocket, looked at it. "Room four," he said.

"Ground floor next door," Dolly said.

"Give me ten minutes to stable my horse," he said, and she nodded with a private little smile. He hurried from the saloon, found the public stable he had noted earlier, and secured a nice roomy corner stall for the Ovaro. He strode back to find the room, saw it held a lamp, a chair, and a double bed, along with a washstand and a pitcher of water. No frills, but clean, and he undressed down to his shorts, hung the gun belt on the bedpost, and opened the door at the knock. Dolly slid into the room, her eyes instantly moving across the contours of his smoothly muscled body, more than approval in her perusal. She unsnapped catches, opened buttons, and the dress fell away as he lowered himself onto the bed. Dolly's full breasts were not as full as they had seemed in the dress, yet they were attractive enough. Her waist a little thick, legs a trifle heavy in the thighs, yet she came to him with an eagerness that was unforced.

Her body came against him, and she gave a little cry of delight as he felt the dark triangle rub against his groin. "This is going to be my lucky night," Dolly murmured.

"Our lucky night, I'm thinking," Fargo said, and she gave a happy little chuckle, brought her breasts up to his face, offering, and he was just beginning to taste one when the sharp knock at the door shattered the moment. Dolly drew back, frowning, and Fargo's brow furrowed as the knock came again, sharper this time. Dolly was still half over him when the door was pushed open. Fargo's jaw dropped as Caroline strode in, her jaw set.

"Get out," she hissed at Dolly, picked up the dress, and threw it at her. "Now, out," she snapped. Dolly rose, holding the dress in front of her as she hurried past Caroline and out of the room.

"What the hell do you think you're doing?" Fargo said from the bed, swinging long legs over the side.

"Protecting my interests," she shot back.

"What I do is my business," Fargo frowned.

"Not if it affects how you do your job. We have to make time starting tomorrow. I don't want you nursing a hangover from too much bourbon and half asleep from too much screwing," Caroline said stiffly.

"You've got your goddamn nerve," Fargo protested.

"It's my prerogative. You're working for me now," she returned haughtily.

"I can fix that," he said, rising, pulling the roll of bills from his jacket. "Here's your damn money."

"You can't do that," she said, unmoved.

"I just did, damn it," he said.

"We made an agreement. You don't go back on your word. That seems to be common knowledge," she said with a note of triumph.

"How do you know that?" Fargo frowned.

"When I heard how good you are as a trailsman, I asked more and heard how good you are with the ladies and bourbon," she said. "I thought it best to rein in that part of you."

He felt the astonishment flooding through him. "That damn inn . . . that's why you sent me there to sleep," he muttered.

"It offered no temptations. When I checked back and found you weren't there, I knew where you'd be," she said.

"You're a piece of work, aren't you," Fargo said.

"Now you can get a good night's sleep. That's all I care about," she said, but he saw her eyes move across his near-naked muscled body.

"I might just go back and find me another girl," he said.

"They won't service you," Caroline said smugly.

"Why the hell not?" he bristled.

"I told them I was counting on you to bring Doc Dodson back. The doc's important to everyone in town, saloon girls, too," she said.

He stared at her. Pale ice. Delicate steel. Through his anger, he felt a grudging admiration for her. "Get the hell out of here," he growled.

"Good night, Fargo," she said as she strode from the room, closing the door gently after her. He lay back on the bed, turned off the lamp, and promised himself to conclude this mission of mercy as quickly as he could.